Y0-CUA-957

Published by Amanda McIntyre
GEORGIA ON MY MIND
AN END OF THE LINE NOVELLA

Copyright © 2017 by Amanda McIntyre
www.amandamcintyresbooks.com

All rights reserved. Except for use in any review, the reproduction or utilization of this work in whole or in part in any form by any electronic, mechanical or other means, now known or hereinafter invented, including xerography, photocopying and recording, or in any information storage or retrieval system, is forbidden without the written permission of the publisher.

This is a work of fiction. Names, characters, places and incidents are either the product of the author's imagination or are used fictitiously, and any resemblance to actual persons, living or dead, business establishments, events or locales is entirely coincidental.

Printed in the USA.

Cover art by Syneca Featherstone

Interior format by

© THE KILLION GROUP, INC.

AMANDA MCINTYRE

Georgia
On My Mind

AN END OF THE LINE NOVELLA

The road leads back to you....

Chapter One

JUSTIN DIDN'T FEEL TEN YEARS older. Then again, there were days when, after wrangling more than one hundred students, he felt ninety. But even that didn't compare to how he felt as he stared at the tiny four-by-six postcard and debated his decision…whether to attend his class reunion in Atlanta.

Justin sighed. The old desk chair squawked as he leaned back, eyeing the invitation. Answering it had been the single most thought on his mind this past week—that, and the memories of the past he'd been fighting to forget.

He'd found sanctuary, if only for a few moments, hidden in the tiny office in the boys' locker room. He was closing in on the end of his third year in the once-booming mining town of End of the Line, Montana, where he taught history and coached the End of the Line Eagles football team.

He propped the invitation against his Eagle's coffee mug—a gift from the team on his birthday. He'd meant to answer the R.S.V.P over the past couple of months, but had conveniently found a number of reasons to procrastinate. A phone call from his mom last night had pushed him a little closer to making a decision, one way or another.

"You get that gray mare settled down?" his mom asked. She was a master at addressing major issues by sliding them through the backdoor of a conversation.

"We did," Justin answered. He sat on the porch swing on his small acreage looking at the late spring sunset. It was a view he would never tire of, but one that he longed to share with someone. And not just anyone—someone by the name of Georgia. He brushed away the thought as he'd done a million times that day. "Michael Greyfeather is an amazing man. He seems to have an instinct when it comes to animals. We're already looking for a forever home for her."

"That's wonderful." There was a pause. "Wouldn't it be nice if we all possessed such a skill when it came to each other?"

Justin chuckled, knowing the reference was pointed to the tense relationship between him and his twin brother, Jake. "I suppose it'd work if you're dealing with an ass."

His mom issued a soft but stern warning. "Justin."

He headed off the question he knew was coming next. "And before you ask, no, I haven't spoken to him."

"Who?" she asked.

"Mom, please. There are few times you call me on a Thursday night. Sundays are your day."

"Fine. I had a call from Jake earlier today and he might have asked whether I'd heard from you."

"Yeah? Why doesn't he just call me?" Justin took a sip of his Jack Daniels. It wasn't something he often chose at the end of the day, but tonight he needed it. Too many nights had been tormented by images of a dark-haired, green-eyed woman he'd thought was out of his system. Damn his photographic memory.

"You know, I can tell you that life's too short."

"Yes, Mom, you can and I'd agree. Too short to dwell on the past. Am I right?" Justin frowned as the whiskey slid down his throat in a slow burn.

"On what you have no power to do anything about, certainly." His mother rivaled Mr. Spock in the logic department. "But this thing between you and your brother…"

"Thing?" Justin straightened, leaning forward as though braced for a fight. "He went behind my back—" Justin paused, forcing himself to bottle his anger. "The point is, maybe things didn't work out between me and Georgia, but Jake—Jake's never mentioned a thing about what he did, much less apologized." He understood how this division between her sons hurt his mom. "I'm sorry, Mom. I didn't want to get into this."

"I know, honey." There was a soft sigh from the other end of the phone. "I don't think it was done as maliciously as you've painted it."

Justin pressed his fingers to his forehead, massaging the dull ache that had started. "Jake rarely does anything, Mom, that doesn't somehow benefit Jake."

"In that regard, he's more like your father just before he died. But understand, Justin, your Dad wasn't always that way. I think the company rooted itself inside your dad and it finally took him."

Justin bit his lip. Georgia had been the one to break things off with him, even before he'd found out what Jake had done.

"I just don't want the same thing to happen to your brother. Faith is a sweet girl. But you, Justin, have always been able to get your brother to balance his perspective."

"At what cost, Mom?" he asked.

"I like to think that things worked out for you, honey. You're working and living in exactly the place you'd always wanted to be. You're content—"

"That's debatable," Justin interjected.

"Surely, you've dated some nice girls since you've been

in End of the Line?"

His doorbell rang, saving him from having to launch into a handful of dates, most of which he botched by mentally comparing them to Georgia. "Mom, my dinner is here. I'll call you later in the week."

"Okay, honey, love you. Go talk to your brother."

He hung up. This damn invitation had blown a hole in his sequestered little life. When he was seated on his porch swing, coffee in hand, catching a brilliant sunset, he'd convinced himself he didn't need any more than this. Trouble was, he'd convinced his brain, not so much his heart.

JUSTIN GLANCED ONCE MORE AT the black-and-white photo of his alma mater. Memories of a rainy afternoon—of him and Georgia—on an old dirt road flickered in his brain. He shook his head. Water under the bridge. He forced his thoughts to the present as he heard the locker room door open and looked up to see his star quarterback over the past three years. "Hey, Eric. How's it going?"

"Hey, Coach. I just stopped by to get this signed." He handed him a pink slip of paper. "My folks want to leave tomorrow after lunch. Dad wants to get an early start on some freakin' family road trip." The teen, now a junior and with a promising future in football, leaned against the doorframe.

The paper fluttered in the breeze left in the wake of the small oscillating fan Justin had brought in and put on the file cabinet to keep the air moving in the locker room.

The boy sighed. "Don't you think that Canada in the summer pretty much looks like Montana?" Eric asked despairingly. "I mean, why now? We've never taken one.

It's the summer before my senior year. I have to take off work, miss doing stuff with my friends—who, by the way, are heading down to Texas."

Justin chuckled softly under his breath as he added his name to the list getting the boy out of tomorrow's study hall. He handed it back, sympathizing with the boy's frustration—parents were impossible to understand. Even so, he felt compelled to offer a bit of 'teacher-like' wisdom. "Hey, your senior year goes pretty fast. Then you'll be heading off to college on a scholarship, no doubt."

Eric shrugged, though his expression remained unenthusiastic. "I'm keeping my grades up, so yeah, I guess."

Justin continued. "Well, then, you'll be starting your life at college, meeting new people, maybe a girl—"

Eric snorted. "I'll have to fight them off."

"Yeah, then the next thing you know, you're married, starting a family…"

"Whoa, Coach, slow your roll. I haven't even met 'the girl' yet." He crooked his fingers for emphasis.

"My point," Justin said, "is that this road trip that seems lame right now might look pretty good in the rearview mirror. You get what I'm saying?"

The teen—his hair grown longer in the off season, along with the scruffy beard—gazed at Justin for a moment. "Yeah, I guess." He lifted a shoulder. "Besides, I've got my laptop and noise-cancelling headphones. I can watch movies, right?"

As a teacher, he could only advise so much. "Right." Justin leaned forward. He dropped his pen on the desk and the invitation fluttered to the teen's feet.

Eric picked it up and casually glanced at it. "So, your class reunion, huh?" he asked, raising a brow as he handed Justin the card. "You going?"

Uncomfortable to be placed on the spot, Justin took

back the card and tossed it on the desk. "Not sure. The timing isn't very good for me."

The boy's mouth turned up in a challenging smile. "What was that you were saying about rearview mirrors?"

Damn. He had been listening. Justin glanced at the card, picked it up, and tapped it against the desk. It'd been a long time since he'd set foot in Atlanta…and he had his reasons. "Go on, Eric. Enjoy this time with your family. Life's too short." His mother's words popped out before he even realized it.

"Yep, like you always tell us, Coach—family is everything." He turned to leave. "Have a good summer. See you at football camp."

"Family is everything," Justin muttered. His mom was right. This had gone on long enough. While he couldn't control all that had happened, he could straighten things out with Jake. Maybe in doing so, he'd be able to put the past to rest in his heart and his brain.

෴

"SORRY I'M LATE. MY PRE-MARRIAGE appointment with a young couple from church went longer than I'd expected." Leslie Cook—now Reverend Leslie Cook of the First Church of Christ in End of the Line, Montana—slid into the booth across from Justin. Considering they lived in such a small town, the two old friends barely saw one another, and lately it had become increasingly difficult even to schedule a dinner together.

"Did you warn them off about the pitfalls of romance?" Justin offered a slanted grin as he glanced over the menu at Betty's diner.

His friend gave him a smile. "Cynicism doesn't look good on you, Justin." She picked up one of the menus

Betty had left.

"Well, look what the cat dragged in. I haven't seen you two out on a date together since you moved here." Betty smiled at one and then the other as she set their wrapped utensils and water on the table. "Glad to see you managed to get this guy out on a real date." Betty chuckled under her breath.

Justin and Leslie looked at her. "It's not a date," they said in unison.

The owner and part-time waitress of the popular eating spot in the little town glanced at each of them and smiled. "Of course, you're not." She pulled out a small tablet and licked the tip of the pencil. "Ok, kids"—because anyone younger than her was considered a kid—"what'll it be? We've got a tuna melt special tonight that comes with my Jerry's seasoned fries, and we have our Thursday night Betty burger topped with pulled pork, coleslaw, and my special Cajun sauce. And you're going to want to save room for dessert because Rebecca just baked up some delicious Dutch apple crumb pies that are to die for."

Justin's stomach growled plaintively. He'd skipped lunch in lieu of an oatmeal cookie he'd found in the teacher's lounge. "What say you, Reverend? My treat," Justin said with a grin.

Betty smiled, but kept her eyes to the notebook.

"It's not a date, Betty," Justin reiterated.

Betty shrugged, then looked at Leslie and grinned. "If I were you I'd order the twelve-ounce steak."

Leslie smiled. "Tuna melt for me, with Jerry's fries. I haven't had those in a long while. Oh, and may I have a house salad, with ranch dressing on the side?"

"You bet." Betty scribbled a few notes and looked at Justin. "How about you, Mr. Reed?"

He closed the menu and handed it to Betty. "A Betty

burger. May I get extra Cajun sauce on the side?"

"Well, that convinces me you aren't on a real date." She grinned. "Coming right up."

After she left, Leslie folded her hands on the table and leaned forward with an expectant look. "Have you made a decision about that reunion?"

She, too, had been haranguing him about attending, but like his Mom, more for resolving his family issues than anything. She had suggested–more than once—that it was best to get things out in the open and to forgive and forget.

Justin glanced up as Betty brought over two salads, glad to stave off answering Leslie's question.

"It's on the house. You looked a bit pale." She scooted the salad toward Justin. "Your specials are coming up." She started to leave and turned on her heel. "I'm sorry, but Reverend, I keep meaning to ask you how many loaves of bread you'll need for the Easter church supper? Now that I have the bakery next door, we'd love to help you any way we can."

Leslie grabbed Betty's hand and squeezed it. "Betty, you are one of the reasons I love this town. You're an angel to offer, but are you sure you have time now with two businesses to run?"

Betty waved her hand dismissively. "It's no problem. I've got a cracker jack team between Rebecca Greyfeather and her granddaughter Emilee, who has been helping after school in the kitchen. And then there's Clay's sister, Julie, who has an amazing head for business. I just get to come in and offer new recipes and brainstorm ideas for new products. I'm the one who is blessed with such a crew." She nudged Leslie's shoulder. "Why, Julie is even working on a website for the bakery to see if we can drum up some online business." She gave Leslie a wink. "But helping you out with feeding the folks in this community and at Miss Ellie's shelter in Billings is my top priority. Besides, we had so many in this town helping out after Jerry's stroke that it's our pleasure to give back any way we can."

Justin smiled as he listened to Betty. It had been her kindness one fateful Saturday morning years ago that had been powerfully influential—in part—to Justin deciding to return years later to End of the Line. His Uncle Roy used to take him and his brother Jake fly fishing once a year at his cabin on the north Yellowstone River. As was tradition, they'd first stop at Betty's for a large breakfast and then make a stop at the town's one and only grocery store to get supplies before heading north. Justin's love of the area—his love for the wide-open spaces, the mountains, being able to breathe—hadn't changed, except that his appreciation had gotten stronger since his youthful days spent on the river, water swirling around his waders as he listened to his uncle's stories. Not a lover of the outdoors, Jake usually opted for sitting on the front porch with his nose in a book, wondering when they were going to eat. Oddly, it'd been his good friend, Leslie—having moved there to take on her first position at First Church of Christ—who had plugged him into the teaching position when it opened in End of the Line.

Diving into their food after it arrived, Justin was relieved when the topic turned from him going to Atlanta to gathering volunteers to serve the Easter dinner. He should have known better. Since meeting her in college his freshman year, he'd never known of anyone like his good friend who could juggle so many projects at once and still be abreast of all the tiny details.

Leslie dabbed her mouth after eating half of her sandwich, sat back, and eyed him. "I'm stuffed. I'll take the rest home." She dabbed a napkin to her mouth and snagged his attention. "Now, about that reunion?"

Speaking of details. Justin took a sip of his water. "I've thought about it."

"You've been doing that the past three months."

Justin leveled her a look. "And I'm still thinking about it." Justin picked off the tomatoes from his burger.

She smiled. "That sounds like you got another call from your mom."

"Maybe," he said with a shrug. Justin sunk his teeth into the warm pretzel bun and nearly groaned. After the rigors of a busy day, there was nothing quite as calming as Betty's comfort food. That might require a few extra sit-ups to be added to his daily routine of chores and exercising horses. He'd also stepped in and had been helping out at the Last Hope Ranch, replacing Clay Saunders who was enjoying being at home with his newborn twin girls born this past December.

He glanced at Leslie, not exactly excited to pick again at the old wound between him and Jake. "Okay, I've spoken to Faith about coming down. I haven't been able to pencil myself in to my brother's schedule as of yet." He shrugged. "Maybe I just need to let it go. Forget all the crap that happened in the past. Stop letting it color our relationship."

She tilted her head. "Crap? Sweetheart, you and I have had many a conversation about what happened at your dad's funeral. You've carried this hurt around for a long time—too long. And it's festering."

That was an understatement. He'd thought he'd be able to accept walking away from Georgia and simply chalk it up to one of life's difficult lessons. But he couldn't do the same with his brother. "I've been waiting for him to make the first move—you know, apologize maybe for going behind my back the way he did.

She reached out and placed her hand on his forearm. "Justin, from what you've told me about your brother, he isn't likely to make the first move. You're going to have to be the better man and get the ball rolling."

Deep down, he knew she was right. After he and Georgia had split, he'd tried to convince himself that what he'd found out, purely by accident—that his Dad, Jake, and Georgia had all been involved in a game of manipulation—no longer mattered. But he'd been lying to himself. He needed closure.

Leslie patted his hand, getting his attention. "You know, this is less about them and more about you, Justin. Clearing this up, confronting Jake, will do a lot toward you being able to move on and find someone new."

Justin considered his friend's wisdom. They'd met in college and had dated a few times, only to discover that they made better friends than lovers. She'd listened to him lament over the Georgia girl who'd gotten away, the one who'd broken his heart. The girl for whom he had been prepared to forego college and marry when there'd been a pregnancy concern; for whom he'd been prepared to settle down, stay in Atlanta, and get a job in his Dad's advertising firm.

He sighed and swiped his hand wearily over his face. "You know, you're right. I need to sit down and have this out with him." He shrugged. "This has less to do with Georgia and more about getting back on an even keel with my brother. Like you said, it's long overdue."

Leslie studied him. "And really, what do you care? I mean, you're clearly over Georgia Langley, right?

Justin met his friend's gaze. "Absolutely."

GEORGIA LOOKED AT THE ARRAY of bills scattered across her father's old desk. The wood was marred, and still reeked of smoke from days gone by when Langley's had allowed smoking inside. She was grateful he wasn't here to see how the urban cowboy bars were putting his beloved bar out of business. Lord knows, she'd tried her best to juggle the mounting bills, but with recent increases to property and business taxes, the upkeep of the tiny business—her father's legacy to his only child—had been suffering in the wake of her son's mounting medical bills.

A knock sounded on the open door. She looked up to see Tank, the ex-marine her father had hired just before he died. He was her bouncer, bartender, manager, and loyal friend. He stood just inside the office door, his muscled arms folded over his faded Metallica T-shirt.

"Hey, kiddo. That was Kevin. He can't make it in tonight." He scratched the now-grey stubble on his chin, which had been darker when her father had found him homeless on the streets in Atlanta and offered him a job.

"Again?" Georgia met the formidable man's steady gaze. "Isn't that the second time this week?"

"Third, lady bug." He offered an I-told-you-so look. "Do you remember me mentioning I didn't think the guy seemed too reliable?"

Georgia sighed. She needed reliable. This filling in at the last minute wasn't fair to Kolby or to her aunt who helped her take care of her son. "Let me see what I can do," she answered, leaning forward to pick up the old rotary dial phone. She'd kept it after taking over the bar, respecting her father's belief that not all customers carried a "a damn cell phone." He never had.

"Sure thing," Tank replied. He hesitated a moment. "You want me to set up an ad in the job-find website?"

Georgia snorted. Thus far, she hadn't had much luck with the applicants from the site. Most were looking for full benefits on part-time work at over minimum wage and were unwilling to work nights, weekends, or holidays. Though these days they closed on major holidays, mainly so she could spend time with her son. "I suppose, if you think it will do any good. Maybe just keep your ears open, maybe tell some of the regulars that we're looking for help."

"Got it," he said as his gaze softened. "Hey, how's that awesome son of yours?"

She smiled at the big man's gentle kindness. When it came to Kolby, Tank was the world's largest teddy bear. "In remission after his last bout of treatments." Georgia crossed her fingers. "Hoping it sticks this time."

The six-foot-three wall of muscle and brawn grinned through his silvery handle-bar moustache. "He's a tough little guy. Learned it from his mama." He glanced at his feet and sniffed once. "Okay, then, I'll get started on that ad."

"Thanks, Tank." The brief conversation had managed to divert her attention briefly from her worry about the mounting bills, but her thoughts swung instead to the cherub-like face of Kolby—her brave little boy. She cradled her head in her hand, forcing herself not to get mentally dragged down by the "what ifs." Together they'd faced the challenge head on since they'd discovered the cancer at the age of three. She opened her eyes and met the twinkling mischief in the photo the two had taken at a recent trip to the zoo. He was far more brave in all of this, never shedding a tear, fewer complaints than she'd ever had, and giving her a smile when she looked sad. He was her little ray of pure, unwavering sunshine.

The shrill ring of the phone jerked her from her

thoughts. She touched her fingers to her lips and tapped the photograph, took a cleansing breath, and picked up the receiver. "Langley's bar, how can I help you today?" She cleared the lump that had formed in her throat from her previous thoughts.

"Just double-checking on the date of our meeting. We're getting tons of responses, which is great," Jolie Harris asserted with her usual, to-the-point brightness. A high school classmate, once head cheerleader, and Georgia's chief nemesis, Jolie now served on the reunion committee.

"I have it on the calendar." Georgia scanned her calendar and noted the red circled around the date.

"Good. I'm anticipating a wonderful turn out given that we missed the five-year mark. There's even the possibility that Jake's brother...what was his name?"

Georgia rolled her eyes. "Justin."

"Oh, right, that's it. I've gotten an email from him that he may show up." There was a pause. "Didn't you two date for a time back in school?" The woman had claws and the bitch attitude down to a science.

"I'll have the lists ready for the meeting," Georgia said, side-stepping Jolie's remark. "I've got to run." She slipped the receiver into the cradle before Jolie could respond.

If all went according to plan, the class reunion could be the break her new catering business needed to supplement the bar's income. Having become aware that many local venues didn't provide bartending services, she decided to answer the need with a portable bar, including staff. The venue being used for the reunion dinner dance was the newly renovated Trolley Barn over in the Inman Park district. Given that she'd much rather attend as a business than socially, she'd agreed to Jolie's query to cater the event. At least this would give her extra capital to stave off the bill hounds for another month.

The downside was the remote possibility that she'd run into Justin Reed. Of course, it'd been ages since their difficult break-up, and she'd gone on to fall in love again with someone else. Still, her heart did a little flip when she thought of her first love.

After their initial break-up at the end of high school, she'd refused his letters, wouldn't return his phone calls. She'd had good reason, given that an arrangement had been made between her father and his. After her pregnancy scare, a surprise visit by his father the summer of their senior year clarified that she would be the one holding Justin back from a promising future. A few years later, after his father's funeral, she'd told him the truth over drinks of what had happened. He hadn't taken the news well and, though she tried to make him see her reasoning, he'd stormed out, believing the worst. Shortly thereafter, she'd heard rumors that his mother had moved to Montana, leaving the family home to Jake and his fiancée.

There were no more phone calls. No more letters. She'd convinced herself that the clean break was for the best and then dove into her responsibilities at the bar to overcompensate for her loss. It wasn't but a few weeks after that she'd heard he'd taken a teaching position in Montana. Though her heart ached that their relationship had ended as it had, she wanted him to be happy and hoped he'd one day find someone his family would accept.

Georgia picked up the calendar and counted the days until the reunion weekend. For all she knew, he had a wife and a tribe of kids by now. Her heart twisted at the thought. She'd felt certain her sacrifice had been the right thing to do, but with the possibility of seeing him again, Georgia's heart ached anew.

She let out a heavy sigh. Had it not been for the fact

that Langley's needed the money, coupled with Jolie's dig that as a local she should participate somehow, she'd have ignored the event altogether.

Georgia sat back and stretched her arms over her head, working out the stress in her shoulders. She needed a breath of fresh air. Walking through to the connecting room, she felt the pang of guilt of her father's sacrifice. When he'd gotten too ill to drive, he'd had the small apartment built at the back of the bar. He'd insisted on working every day at the bar—cleaning, visiting with patrons, taking care of the bills—all the things she now had taken on.

"I'm sorry, Dad," she said as she picked up the last photo they'd taken together. They were both smiling, unaware of how the world would come crashing down around them in a few short days. He died two weeks after the photo, leaving her the bar. She'd found solace in the arms of a country western singer who'd played the bar while touring with his band. And less than two weeks later, she'd lost him, too, in a horrific accident.

The pang of loss threatened to overwhelm her as it did when she dwelled on it. She pushed open the door leading out to a small porch that looked out on the tall Georgia pine at the back of the property. Her father used to come out here when he had a problem, something he needed to work out alone. He built the porch purposely facing the west, so he could see the sunset each night. It was his favorite time of day. He'd insisted that he should be buried at dusk.

Georgia eased into the old rocker that was her father's and looked out across the darkening sky. She'd spent a lot of sunsets since out here on this very porch searching the twilight sky, asking God for answers to her questions about Kolby's illness and his father's untimely death, as well as the disease that taken her father away too soon.

She had no answers yet to any of her questions—perhaps she never would.

The scent of pork roasting in the smoker outside the back door tickled her nose. She leaned back and took in a deep breath of the night air mixed with the earthy scent of Georgia pine coming from the grove of trees that her father had battled to keep when builders suggested they be taken down.

Her Dad had chosen this location and built the bar in homage to "southern hospitality" he felt was lacking in the city. It sat on the outskirts of the posh Atlanta suburbs, and had over time become the favorite of both blue-collar workers and the business elite of Atlanta. They came from miles around to savor a place to relax, enjoy a little southern comfort, and tap their feet to the music of up-and-coming country-western singers crisscrossing the honky-tonks in search of fame and fortune.

Georgia had started washing dishes at the age of fourteen and worked her way up to waitressing, and eventually to the business side of the bar. It's where she'd first seen Justin Reed at the age of eighteen, trying to sneak in with his twin brother and a couple of friends to see one of the bands playing one early fall weekend. Tank had thwarted their plan immediately, calling them on their ruse by threatening to call one of the fathers to confirm their ages. It would be a couple of weeks later that she'd see him again. Georgia smiled as her thoughts drifted back to that fall evening long ago…

GEORGIA HAD NEVER HUNG WITH the popular crowd. In truth, she'd found them boring and the majority of them spoiled. She preferred the artistic variety—music and theater students who hung out after school in the art room. Which only lent itself to confusion as to why she seemed to have a weird obsession for Justin Reed, a senior. He was the quieter of the twin brothers—both on the football team. Jake was the star quarterback. Justin—quicker on his feet—was one of the team's top receivers. She'd gone with a friend to the homecoming game—a first in the history of her school career—but it was curiosity that drew her to observe the guy who'd inadvertently tossed her a friendly if not entirely humiliated smile as Tank escorted him from her father's bar. Her friend, who happened to know one of the players with whom she had a "study arrangement", had invited her to the bonfire after the game. She'd begged Georgia to go at the last possible moment, planting the seed of possibility that Justin Reed just might show.

That was all the incentive she'd needed. Still, she wasn't about to reveal her hand entirely, even to her friend. "Okay, fine. I'll hate it. All those snotty kids thinking they're so much better than everyone, getting by with their kegs and coolers." She glanced at her friend and chuckled. "Guess someone has to keep their eye on you."

Her friend had smiled.

Later that night, Georgia had begun to regret her decision. She sat alone on an old log near the bonfire. The hoodie under her jean jacket barely covered enough to keep her warm from the chilly autumn night. Everyone around her was drinking, it seemed, laughing and nudging one another with dares to go visit the old house in the woods reported to have once been used as a hospital during the Civil War and was now haunted by those who'd died there. But Georgia knew it was primarily a dark, private place for kids to go make out. That's where her friend and her study buddy had run off to, deserting her at the bonfire.

Georgia huddled as close to the fire as she could, watching the marshmallow on the end of her stick blacken to ash.

"Hey, it's about damn time the rest of you got here," came a yell from the shadows.

Jake Reed, as handsome as he was vocal, hopped from the old pickup truck and punched his fist into the air, emitting a tribal yell of victory. Those who'd been riding in the bed of the truck leapt over the side, following suit. The letter-jacketed cluster of athletes left one of their own in their wake.

Justin Reed.

Georgia watched as he stepped out of the driver's side and pocketed his keys. She'd been there for nearly forty minutes without so much as a nod from anyone and had all but convinced herself that she was invisible to those she had no social connection to, so why would he even notice her staring at him? She staked her life that he was the designated driver tonight for his rowdy brother and his friends. They all beelined after Jake, who was heading for the keg.

She observed Justin stuff his hand in his pocket and scan the crowd of fifty or so homecoming revelers before pulling out his cell phone glancing at the time. She caught his heavy sigh followed by an eyeroll as he watched his brother, red Solo cup in hand, drop his arm around Jolie, the head cheerleader.

She was about to go back to her dying marshmallow when his gaze crossed path with hers. Okay, she might have claimed creative license when it seemed his eyes locked with hers with the heat of the fire crackling between them. Georgia's heart faltered—what the hell?

—which was an absurdity given that this guy was not in her league. Not even close. Oh, sure, she was worth it. She was a badass. Daughter of the owner of one of Atlanta's hottest honky-tonks. She chuckled softly, doubting Justin Reed had ever met anyone outside his upper crust, country-club status.

Georgia held his gaze as he walked over and sat down on the log next to her. She looked away, then focused on tossing her burnt blob of marshmallow into the fire—stick and all.

"Some game, huh?" he said. He looked around as though mildly curious if anyone noticed him slumming it with the ghost in their midst.

Georgia didn't respond, but poked at the fire, waiting for him to decide to leave.

After a moment, he chuckled as though she'd said something funny. "I can't believe that last play, can you? Damn, I was lucky that Jake found me after I screwed up the play." He shrugged. "I guess the important thing is we won, right?" He glanced at her. "You remember the play I'm talking about, right?"

He was adorable. Sweet. Probably lived in one of those ritzy districts where they had scheduled neighborhood potlucks every Friday night during the summer. "I don't like football as a rule," she said, forcing herself to look into those amazing blue eyes.

She wanted to kick herself for the flicker of hurt she saw pass through his gaze. He frowned and eyed her.

"Really, you don't ever go to any of the games? Who doesn't go to football games—especially homecoming?"

He gave her a lop-sided grin to show he was teasing her. This time, however, she was close enough to see the cute dimple that accompanied the smile.

"You do go to this school though, right?

Yeah, okay, maybe she deserved that. Still, it pissed her off. She pushed to her feet, ready to walk back to town if need be. He grabbed her arm.

"Hey, come on. It's just that you seem familiar." He slid his hand in hers, tugging on it until she sat back down. "I promise, we don't have to talk about football."

Georgia glanced at his handsome face. Those crystal blue eyes all but twinkled in the firelight. She wasn't sure he'd keep his promise, but it was for certain that, right then and there, she'd fallen for Justin Reed—hard.

They talked, and Georgia found it surprisingly easy. So much so that later that night, when he'd dared her to go with him and a few others to the abandoned Stoneville house, promising he'd not leave her side and she didn't need to be afraid, she agreed. The challenge that she couldn't handle fear is what had pushed her to go. When, at one point on the dark trail through the woods, two of the guys veered off to create spooky noises for those going on, Justin pulled her behind a large oak and explained what was about to happen to those who'd walked ahead.

"And should I be afraid of what's going to happen to me all alone with you out here in the dark?" she'd asked, touching her hand to his cheek.

He'd kissed her as she'd hoped, cautiously at first. Tentative. Unsure of his sexual prowess. Georgia had wondered if he'd ever kissed a girl before.

Maybe it was the night, the company, maybe the half cup of beer that left a pleasant buzz to her brain. But she grabbed the back of his head, infused with the need to taste his lips on hers. She'd pined after him silently for weeks, sneaking glimpses of him as he walked through the halls at school, their shoulders briefly touching once in the crowd between classes. He hadn't noticed, but she hadn't washed that shirt for a month after.

"Wow," he said softly, resting his forehead against hers. He licked his lips and searched her eyes.

"I saw you that night at my dad's bar," she confessed.

His gaze narrowed. "That's right, at Langley's." His hand slid down, drawing her hips to his. He grinned. "You were bussing tables, as I recall, that night. I knew we'd met before." He touched his lips to hers.

"Not really met," she said between his persistent kisses.

"Georgia, right?" he nuzzled the spot below her ear.

Chills raced down her spine, to her knees and everywhere in between. He knew her name? "Yeah, Georgia Anne," she whispered, drugged by his charm.

"Georgia Anne," he repeated with a smile as he studied her face. "I think you and I are going to get to know each other a whole lot more. What do you say?"

She fisted his jacket and dragged him closer, delighting in the low growl as she pulled him into another fiery kiss.

So began the season of their senior year—a year of unbridled, youthful passion. Oblivious to anyone but each other, they spent every moment together, defying anyone to call what they had anything but the "real deal." That summer before he was to leave for college was seared in her memory. One rainy afternoon on an old deserted dirt road, they'd both lost their virginity in the cab of his beat up pick-up truck.

☙

"HEY, GEORGIA."

Shaken by her bartender's authoritative voice, Georgia shook herself from the ancient memories.

"It's that distributor again." Tank held the side door open. "Wants to talk with you about the order you placed earlier this week."

Her body tingled still from her previous thoughts. She blew out a sigh and looked up at the stars beginning to dot the night sky, realizing how she'd lost track of time. "I'm on my way."

Chapter Two

JUSTIN SAT ON THE TARMAC, staring out the plane's window. He was on the last leg of his flight that took him from Omaha to Chicago and finally on to Atlanta. He'd waited three hours at Midway for adverse weather to pass through the city. The plane was full. A few seats back a baby was being soothed by a parent. His nerves were stretched thin, and two hours ago, he'd started contemplating again the wisdom of going back home. It had been three years since he'd set foot in his brother's home. Three years since he'd visited his father's grave. His eyes drifted shut as the plane began to taxi for take-off.

He'd seen her during the service at the cemetery, standing near an old oak tree at the edge of the road. She held an umbrella. Her hand lifted with a tissue to dab at her eye, then she climbed into the small car he remembered she drove back in high school.

Unsure why, he left, following her into the deserted Langley's parking lot, and caught up with her as she unlocked the front door.

She turned, startled to see him. "Justin."

"Hi," he said, unable to stop staring at how she'd become even more beautiful since the last time he'd seen her. Her dark hair was swept up, exposing the gentle curve of her neck. He blinked, pulling himself from wondering whether her skin still smelled of

lavender and iris.

"I was sorry to hear about your dad," she said. Her eyes searched his. "I could use a drink. How about you?"

Justin followed her back to the small apartment off the back of the bar.

"I've been living here while trying to get the bar back up and running after Dad died," she said, slipping off her black heels. She wore a dark gray sleeveless shift that followed her curves.

"I didn't hear about your dad, I'm sorry." Suddenly his life seemed so distant from hers.

She poured him a finger of scotch and ushered him to sit. "It's okay. It's been a couple of years now. At least he's not suffering anymore." She smiled sadly and held up her glass. "To our fathers."

Justin watched as she tipped hers back like a shot. He followed suit. Three glasses later, they found themselves traveling down memory lane, laughing at the good times, smiling through the awkward silences when their gazes would meet and the past ignited between them. Maybe it was guilt, grief—a need to be close to someone who understood him. He took her glass and leaned in to kiss her. The taste of whiskey was on her tongue, her lips. It wasn't slow and easy, once the floodgates of passion opened. Barely out of their dress clothes, all inhibitions were flung aside. Driving one another blindly to the precipice of oblivion, she clung to him, her soft, encouraging words infusing his soul with life.

Later, she'd taken him to her bed, where the world itself seemed to fade away. Into the wee hours of the morning they explored one another—satisfying, pleasuring, whispering words spoken in passion, urging each other until they fell asleep in each other's arms.

As the first fingers of dawn crept through the window,

they'd lain with a sheet covering them both, her head resting on his shoulder. He'd dozed off and on for an hour, not wanting to miss a moment shared with her. Picking up her hand, he'd rubbed his thumb over her slender fingers, relishing how his body remembered her gentle exploration. "You know, I never understood what happened between us. I mean, I know you didn't want me to give up going to college. But I guess we were both pretty young."

She rose on her elbow, giving him an inquisitive look.

"What?" he said.

"Your father never said anything?"

Justin sat up as Georgia climbed out of bed, wrapped a robe around her, and walked back to the living room. Confused, he slipped on his pants and followed her.

"What are you talking about?" A cold dread formed a pit in his stomach at the thought of his manipulative father and what he might have done.

She held her clothes in front of her, obviously hesitant to speak openly.

"Georgia? What about my dad?"

"Well, I guess it doesn't matter much now." She offered him a weak smile. "He paid a visit to me and my dad that summer. You'd already been accepted to numerous colleges and were still deciding." She curled a strand of hair behind her ear. "It was around the time when I had that little pregnancy scare."

Justin sat down on the arm of the sofa. He had a feeling he wasn't going to like what he heard.

"Before I go any further, understand that it was probably the best for everyone involved. We were both too young. Things between us had moved too fast—and, in truth, it was mostly physical." She caught her lip with her teeth, uncertain to continue.

"Bull," he muttered. Even though, deep down, he knew she was right.

"Your dad," she started, "came to see mine one afternoon. He made a lucrative offer to my father and asked me to stay away from you." She looked down. "To be fair, I had already planned to break things off, simply because I didn't want you to give up your future for me. I couldn't have lived with myself." She shrugged, darting him a look. "And my dad, his health was getting worse. I knew he was going to need me. I'm all he had, Justin."

He shook his head, trying to understand what she was telling him. "You mean to tell me that my dad paid yours to force you to break up with me?" He narrowed his gaze on her.

"I told him no. My dad told him no." She hugged herself, having a difficult time getting through this. "I told him he didn't need to pay anyone, that I'd already decided to break things off with you."

Justin felt as though he'd been smacked with a fast ball from left field. He swallowed, trying make sense of what he was hearing. "I don't understand—how'd he know about us? The man never paid any attention to me—Jake was his favorite. The kid could do no wrong." It dawned on him then how his father discovered about his relationship with Georgia.

He met Georgia's gaze. "Jake told him."

"Does it matter now, Justin?" She sat down at the opposite end of the couch. "Your dad's gone. My dad's gone."

He glanced at her. "So, you're okay with how things turned out?"

"I'm the one who should be offended here, aren't I? It was your father who came here ready to strike a deal. And your brother who instigated it."

Jesus. She might as well have driven a dagger in his heart. Justin rose and slipped into his shirt and shoes, and started to leave.

She stopped him.

"I'm sorry that you had to find out this way."

"And that you never answered my letters, returned my calls."

"It was part of what I promised." *She clamped her hand on his arm. "Justin, it was better the way things turned out."*

"So, what was this?" He jerked his arm away. "A pity fuck?" He shook his head. Though there was a measure of truth to her reason, the fact remained that she hadn't been truthful with him—and more, his own brother had gone behind his back and never once mentioned it, much less apologized. Then again, Jake was like his dad in that he very rarely apologized for anything. The bastard. He was going to kill him.

Hurt flickered in her gaze. She stepped away. Her chin lifted in defiance. "Goodbye, Justin."

Pride churned his gut. She didn't have to say it more than once.

౿ళ

A GENTLE NUDGE ON HIS SHOULDER brought him fully awake. He looked up into the kind eyes of the flight attendant. "Please bring your seat to a full and upright position. We're preparing to land in Atlanta."

The dream lingered in his brain and Justin glanced out the window, seeing the familiar landscape below. Life had moved so fast in the days following that there'd been no time to speak privately to Jake. He and Faith had taken off on a cruise to explore possible destination weddings venues, while he helped his mom move to eastern Montana to help care for her sister. After acquiring a new job teaching and taking on coaching, he'd all but left the pain and heartache of Atlanta behind.

A sudden jerk clenched at his stomach as the wheels touched the ground. His fingers curled around the arm of the chair as the plane sped like a banshee down the runway. Trapped inside, its passengers could only hope that, when all was said and done, they'd arrive in one piece, no worse for the wear.

That's exactly how he felt about this weekend.

&

"JUSTIN, IT'S BEEN A LONG time. Come on in." The lanky blonde with deep, brown eyes stepped aside, holding open the door that, for eighteen years of his life, he'd carried a key.

"Thanks, Faith," he said. "That traffic is more brutal than I remember." He dropped his luggage in the foyer where once he'd dropped his gym bag—much to his father's disdain.

"It's so good to see you." His brother's beautiful wife reached out and pulled him into a warm embrace. Jake had met Faith just after he'd started as vice-president of Andrew Wade Reed's successful advertising firm. That was a year before their dad had been found dead of a heart attack in his private lavatory off his luxury top-floor office. A year later Faith and Jake had joined a few friends and family members in St. Croix where they were married in a lavish, private ceremony. Both had been highly competitive in their fields—now Faith stayed at home managing the house, the Buckhead neighborhood association, and a half-dozen or so other philanthropic groups that made her husband look good to his peers in the community. Jake took his business seriously and Justin just hoped that the firm wouldn't swallow him whole, the same as it had their father.

"It's good to see you, too." Justin glanced over her shoulder. "Where's that brother of mine?" He glanced at his watch. It was almost nine o'clock on a Wednesday night. He sniffed, catching the lingering scent of a pot roast wafting from the kitchen.

"Oh, Jake called to say that he was running a little late. They're closing a big deal today with an important client."

Justin brushed off Faith's obvious embarrassment that Jake hadn't bothered to give Justin a call himself. "Is that a roast I smell?" He changed the topic.

His sister-in-law's eyes lit up. "It is. I've had it in all day. Are your hungry?"

"Starving." Justin removed the casual suit jacket he'd worn on the plane. "Those pretzels and peanuts just don't cut it." He reached out and blindly dropped his coat on the row of hooks he'd known to be on the wall to the left for years. His jacket slid down the wall in a lifeless heap. Justin smiled and grabbed it before Faith. "Old habit," he said with a grin, but he couldn't shake the feeling that he was a stranger in his childhood home.

Faith held out her hand "It's okay. Justin didn't like the clutter in the foyer." She turned around and hung it on the bannister post of the steps leading to the second floor. "That way you can grab it before you head up to the guest…er, your room."

He nodded, determined not to let his awkwardness show. "I'm sure you guys have done great things with the place." Justin followed her past the stairwell and down the corridor connecting the foyer to the back of the house, specifically the kitchen—or what used to be the kitchen. He blinked against the harsh glare of clinical lighting made all the more so by the sterile black and white of all the appliances, cabinets, and flooring. It gleamed with the luster of a new car showroom. He couldn't imagine their mom, Sylvia Reed, would appreciate all the modern touches of granite and steel. Suffice it to say, it was no longer the cozy place where they'd done their homework at the dining room table under the watchful eye of their mom. He squinted against the sterile brightness and rubbed his eyes, already burning with fatigue from his early morning flight and several layovers in airports.

"I know it's not how you remember it, Justin. Jake decided he wanted a more—"

"Modern look?" Justin filled in with a smile.

Faith shrugged. "You know how your brother loves urban industrial."

Justin slid onto the chrome barstool, one of four alongside the giant granite-topped work island placed in the center of the kitchen. "He always preferred glass and steel…just like Dad." Until he'd moved away, Justin hadn't realized how polar opposite they were in so many ways. Justin had followed their mom out to help on the rescue ranch on weekends, while Jake loved going to the office downtown with their Dad.

Faith got a plate out and served up a plate of steaming roast, potatoes, and a variety of vegetables from the Crock Pot. Reaching beneath a napkin covering a basket, she produced two crescent rolls and placed them on his plate.

His mouth watered as she slid the meal across to him, along with a bundle of napkin-wrapped utensils. "That's handy." He held up the enclosed fork and knife.

"Jake likes things to be organized," she said with a smile over her shoulder.

Justin chuckled under his breath and thought you could add "controlling" to the list, as well.

He took a bite and savored the meat cooked to perfection. He noted that Faith had poured him a glass of sweet tea and she leaned against the counter now, sipping her own.

"You're not joining me?" he asked.

She smiled. "You look pretty famished. How is it?"

"Fantastic," he mumbled, stuffing another forkful into his mouth. It rivaled Betty's fare at the diner in End of the Line, and that was saying a lot.

"Jake prefers I wait on him." She took a drink of her tea. "I'm sure he won't be much longer."

Justin wanted to ask if it was commonplace for them to eat so late in the evening. He remembered a few times when dinner at home would run late due to their dad, but it never seemed to go past seven. "Well, if he doesn't get here soon, there may not be any left. This is delicious, Faith."

Her smile in return was genuine. "You know, I bought a pie over at the bakery in Inman Park."

Justin leaned back, eyeing her. "Seriously, is it a Georgia peach pie?"

"None other," she said with a pleased smile.

"Okay, now you're just trying to fatten me up." Justin leaned forward and dug into the parslied potatoes on his plate. He glanced up to see her cheeks cast with a rosy glow. He wondered how often Jake complimented his wife's cooking.

"Not at all," she said. "It's just nice to see a man with an appetite."

Justin slathered butter on a roll as he spoke. "Has my brother gone vegan?"

"No." She waved off his comment. "He's just extremely careful to measure out ounces and carbs. He goes to the gym every Saturday morning with a personal trainer."

Justin usually worked out with his players, but lately he'd been getting a workout just helping at the ranch and riding the horses. He washed down the roll with a swallow of rich, hot coffee. The fresh brew calmed him like hot tea did for some. He'd always been able to sleep well even after drinking coffee this late into the evening. "Personal trainer, huh?" He glanced at Faith. "Did he give up drinking, too?" He couldn't imagine Jake giving up his bourbon, especially with a social event coming up.

Faith raised her brow and set her glass down as the front door opened. "That and work are the two things that he never measures," she said, quietly darting a guarded look at Justin. "Hello, honey. Glad to have you home. Justin is here."

He heard the muffled sound of urgent whispers just before Jake appeared all smiles around the corner of the kitchen. "Well, look who's decided to pay his brother a visit. I knew it was you when I saw that damn red truck in the driveway. Thought you'd have gotten that out of your system by now."

Justin stood and offered Jake a brief embrace. "Aw, now." He gave his brother a smartass grin. "I promise not to run over that little BMW of yours."

Jake held him at arm's length and eyed him. "Geez, how long's it been?"

Justin shrugged. "Long enough. How are you, anyway?" He playfully punched his brother's shoulder. Jake had changed physically since he'd seen him last at their wedding. He was leaner, harder looking. He had a competitive glint in his eyes—which, he noted, were rimmed with dark circles. But his smile, that-let-me-sell-you-a-special-deal brilliance, was the same. As was his cantankerous attitude.

"Did you eat all of my supper?" Jake asked with a lopsided grin as he lifted the crockpot lid.

Justin slid back onto the barstool. "Was on my way. Good thing you got here when you did. Your wife cooked an amazing supper." He expected the two would serve themselves and join him at the island, but instead Jake reached into the cabinet and pulled down a bottle of bourbon. He tipped it into a glass. "Oh, honey, I forgot to mention I picked up a sandwich at that little deli near work. I'm just going to grab a drink and go visit with my long-lost brother outside. It's a beautiful night. Why don't you join us after you've gotten things cleaned up in here?" Jake kissed Faith's forehead.

Justin cringed inside, his heart twisting for his beautiful, capable sister-in-law. "I think I'll go ahead and finish in here if it's all the same to you," Justin said.

Jake shrugged. "Come on out when you're through, then." Jake walked through the French doors leading outside.

Faith looked at him. "Thank you, I appreciate what you did there. Jake can be an ass sometimes."

"Hoped he'd grown out of that a bit," Justin said, glancing at his sister-in-law.

Faith braced her hands on the countertop. "He carries a lot of the weight of the company on his shoulders. Sometimes, it gets shoveled out here. I can take it."

Justin wanted to say that as much of a workaholic as their father had been, he'd never been disrespectful to his wife—at least, not in front of him and Jake. Justin finished his last bite and grabbed his coffee cup. Standing, he walked around the island and gave Faith a hug. "That was the best meal I've had in a long time, thank you." He looked at her. "You need some help in here?"

Faith smiled. "Go on. You two have a lot to catch up on. Besides, I've got to do some last-minute preparation on a dinner I'm serving here tomorrow night."

"Okay, you're sure?"

"Really. You're very sweet to ask, Justin." She leaned forward and kissed his cheek.

"Hey, I leave the room for a minute and look what

happens." Jake stood in the shadows of the open-ended kitchen. He had a wide smile as he stepped into the light. "Just came to freshen my drink." He grabbed the bourbon bottle and poured his glass half full. "Did you say your dinner was tomorrow night, honey?" he said over his shoulder.

"Yes," she answered.

"Good, the reunion committee wanted to meet to go over the last-minute plans." He slapped Justin on the shoulder. "Come on outside, I want to show you something."

Justin walked ahead of his brother.

"Yeah, Jolie Harris—you remember her, the head cheerleader—boy, has she been chomping at the bit to see you since she heard you coming back."

Jake's words were lost as Justin came to a full stop at the sight before him. He blinked to make sure he wasn't hallucinating. What had once been a lush backyard with well-maintained, carefully thought-out flower gardens was now swallowed up by an Italian stone floor and a massive arched roof of rough hewn beams. Two rustic outdoor chandeliers hung from crossbeams at opposite ends of the outdoor living area. A brick oven with an outdoor built-in grill graced one end with a massive table for eight. A kidney-shaped pool surrounded by lights lay sparkling beyond.

He stood there, realizing with sudden clarity that the home he'd grown up in—the old tree he'd once climbed, the yard where he'd pitched his first pup tent—was gone. Nothing now but a memory.

"What do you think?" Jake plopped down on the wicker and brown leather couch—part of a seating area that would easily accommodate a dozen people.

"What happened to the yard?" His feet were like clay.

Jesus. How their Mom had slaved over those flowers. They were the prize roses of the neighborhood's spring garden club.

"Really? That's all you've got to say?" Jake shook his head as he settled back and propped his feet on the glass and wicker coffee table.

Oh, hell, no. Justin glanced at his brother, aware that any hope he had to confront his brother politely had flown right out the window.

"Did you ask Mom about taking out her roses?" he asked.

Jake chuckled. "It's my house now, Justin. Besides, when she left she said I could do whatever I needed to make it a home for me and Faith."

Justin shook his head. "And you most certainly have. I hardly recognize the place."

Justin's gaze scanned the elaborate yard. Their dad would have killed for this set-up, but their mom wouldn't have it. She wanted an area meant for a family.

"So, is that all you have to say?" Jake grinned.

"If this"—he swept a wave across the view—"is your idea of happiness, and Faith's, then good for you." He sat his cup down and looked at his very corporate-looking brother, complete with his starched shirt, pressed black slacks, and loosened tie. "I just don't happen to think a person needs all of this to be successful."

Jake raised his brow. "That truck is evidence of that," he smirked.

The niggling anger that had been stuffed deep inside Justin began to rise. "Just because I don't happen to buy into your corporate lifestyle doesn't mean I'm not happy or successful." He snatched the bourbon from his surprised brother's hand, tossing it back in one gulp. He sucked in a deep breath as the burn fueled his resolve. This lavish décor, how he treated his wife, his inability to show any fuckin' compassion whatsoever for their mom's years of hard work on her flowers, and more to the point, the fact he'd gone behind his back and never bothered to mention it set his teeth on edge. He paced a few steps, attempting to corral his thoughts as opposed to just beating the smug look off his brother's face.

Jake looked at him with a dubious expression, further fanning Justin's ire. He pointed the empty glass at his brother. "And you know what else, Jake? You need to start treating your wife like a human being instead of one of your office flunkies."

Jake's gaze narrowed. "My marriage is none of your business."

"You're one to talk about interfering in other people's business." He shook his head. "What the hell. You just don't get it, do? Because you've always been so damn full of yourself. Hell, man, you don't even see what you have right in front of you."

"Oh, there it is. The high and mighty Saint Justin." He snorted.

Something snapped inside him. In two long strides, Justin hauled his brother from the chair, and, with both fists gripping the front of his shirt, pressed his nose to Jake's. "It's better than being an asshole."

"What the fuck is eating you?" Jake glared at him.

Justin's hands trembled with frustration. He searched his brother's eyes and realized he likely didn't even remember a thing. "You know, for a long time I held out hope that once you got settled down, you'd remember and apologize for how you treated me—how you treated Georgia."

"Georgia?" Jake appeared genuinely surprised. "Are you still carrying around a torch for that girl?"

Justin dropped his grasp, shoving his brother away. He

held up his hands. "I'm going to check in someplace else for the weekend." He started toward the door.

Faith blocked his way.

"Oh, no. You'll do no such thing. The two of have something you need to get straightened out between you. I'm sick of it. Your mom is sick of it. The whole damn world is sick of it. So"—she pointed at Justin and then her husband, who now stood looking at her—"you two are going to get this resolved this weekend. Or I'm going to drown you both in that lovely pool. And don't think I won't."

A very contrite Jake smiled and stepped around Justin, putting his arm around his wife's waist. "I'm sorry, baby. You know how I get when I'm under pressure."

She eyed him. "We talked about this, Jacob."

He nodded. "We did, darlin'." Jake glanced over his shoulder. "And we'll get things straightened out, I promise. Right now, I think we're all a little tired."

"Jake," came a stern warning from his wife.

"I promise, baby. It's going to be fine." He glanced at Justin. "Right, Justin?

She tipped her head and studied him, then glanced at Justin. "You'll stay, promise?"

Justin sighed and then nodded. "I'm going to take a little drive. If you could give me a spare key—you guys don't need to wait up."

A grin crawled up his brother's face. "No plans to, bro." He hugged his wife's waist and led her away.

A few moments later, Justin found himself driving past what used to be Georgia Langley's house. It appeared smaller than he remembered. There were no lights on, but at just past midnight few of the houses had lights on. He pulled up to the curb and his memory played tricks on him, remembering that summer, seeing Georgia in her cut-off shorts, flimsy tank top, and a hooded sweatshirt hooked over one arm as she climbed out of the second-story window and shimmied down the lattice-work trellis from the porch roof. Breathing heavily by the time she opened the door, she'd toss him a sexy smile. "This better be worth it, Justin Reed," she'd say, sliding into the front seat of the old pickup he'd bought by mucking stalls at the equine ranch a few miles out of town.

Justin stared into the shadows, swearing he could—even now—smell the scent of her skin, remembering how her sexy smile could arouse him.

They'd graduated from high school and, for him, at least, college lay on the horizon, but the summer seemed to stretch out long and lazily before them. He'd lost his virginity, as had she, in his truck. He remembered the rain on the roof, remembered how scared he was. Had his condom not torn and she'd not hastily waved off any concern, it might have been more of a magical first time for them both. As it turned out, he came too soon, she wasn't sure if she'd had an orgasm, and both had been left with the startling realization that she could get pregnant. And, in fact, when she'd told him a few weeks later that she was late, he'd immediately began preparations to forego college, get married, and find a job in his father's firm.

That's when things went south. Next thing he knew, she'd broken up with him with little to no explanation.

༺

JUSTIN PULLED HIS GAZE FROM the house and started the truck. He rubbed the ache that had crawled its way into his chest. He'd loved Georgia with every fiber of his youthful heart and still, after all this time, wasn't sure that he'd ever be completely over her.

The next night, Jake suggested he drive to the reunion meeting. He'd gotten home later than expected and had hopped in at the last-minute, directing Justin what route to take. The air between them was tense, but hospitable. It was Jake who first broke the silence. "Hey, I'm glad you decided to stay. Oh, wait. Don't miss our turn. The drive is up there, on the right."

Jake pulled into the familiar gravel lot. "You're not serious?" Justin shot a look at his brother.

"Hey, if it's a problem"—Jake pulled out his cell phone—"I can call the others and let them know the meeting place has been changed."

He stared at the new green neon sign glowing Langley's. He hadn't turned off the ignition yet.

"Hey, to be fair, I didn't schedule it here. Jolie Harris did. She said we needed to meet here, because of Georgia."

Justin's gaze snapped to Jake's. "Georgia?"

His brother raised a brow. "You don't read your emails, do you?"

Justin kicked himself silently for not reading them, but to be fair he'd not even planned on coming until the last minute. This was something he was going to have to suck up and deal with.

"Georgia is trying to start up a catering business, I guess to help supplement costs at the bar." Jake shrugged. "Jolie found out and called her because we needed a couple of bars set up at the reception Saturday night. She apparently gave Jolie a good deal. It's a win-win for everyone."

"I'll bet," Justin mumbled, pocketing his keys as he climbed out of the truck. And the hits just kept coming. Justin walked a few paces behind his brother as the memory of the exotic wedding and the news shared with him by their drunk friend, Mac, washed over him—news that

Jake had been hitting on Georgia at Jake's bachelor party, and that she'd been seen getting into Jake's car and heading to a seedy motel down the road with him. He'd been surprised, a little hurt—but what hurt more was Jake's dismissal of the rumor. That was the reason he'd come back to Atlanta, to set things right with his brother. After the last encounter he'd had with Georgia, he wasn't prepared to face her again.

Chewing the inside of his lip, he followed Jake inside, weaving through an array of empty tables to the far back where several of his classmates sat at a large, round table.

Jake took a seat next to Mac, who smiled and stood, shaking both Justin's and Jake's hands.

Madeline Hurt—Maddie for short—was busy peering over a list, her red reading glasses perched at the end of her nose. She glanced up and smiled, holding up her arm to embrace Justin as he leaned down to accept her hug.

"Justin, it's good to see you. I'm glad you could make it," she said in the same authoritative tone she'd always possessed.

"Middle school principal, right?" He smiled as he sat down between her and an empty chair.

Her dark eyes twinkled as her smile widened. "We've probably got a lot of war stories we could share, eh?"

"Well, as I live and breathe, if it isn't Justin Reed, in the flesh."

Justin saw a bare arm set an appletini on the table and turned just in time to get a face full of cleavage as Jolie leaned down and draped her arms around his neck. She wiggled her breasts against him in a far-too-intimate hug.

"I was afraid you'd be a no-show." She kissed his cheek and pulled the empty chair closer to his before sitting down. "It's so damn good to see you, darlin'."

Her pure southern drawl slid over him. His gaze met

Jake's who sat across the table, his brother's smile saying, "I told you so."

"Good to see you, Jolie." Justin grabbed her hand, now firmly gripping his thigh, and brought it to his lips.

"Oh, my, chivalry does still exist." She giggled with a little flourish of her hand.

Justin glanced around the bar and noted it was quiet for a Thursday night. Tank—who appeared as big and as formidable as he remembered—stood next to a young man behind the bar, tutoring him in using the tap.

"Well, hey, I'm parched." He stood and squeezed himself between his chair and Jolie's. "Anyone need anything?" he asked, pointing to those around the table. His gaze came to rest on Jolie, whose eyes traveled from the lateral view of his crotch to his eyes. She turned her face up, smiling through ruby red lips.

"I've already had two of these little gems tonight." She eyed her peers. "I may need one of you gentlemen to take me home tonight if I have one more." She slid a look back at Justin. "Besides, what I'd like they don't serve at a bar."

Justin caught Mac's muffled chuckle. Jake just turned his head to hide his grin.

"I'll take that as a no, then," he said, grateful for the opportunity to put some distance between him and Jolie's tentacles. He walked up to the bar, eyeing the selections posted, when his eye caught a movement. He saw Georgia walk in through the back hallway and sit down at the office desk. His heart stopped, while everything else—fueled from his last memories of them together—came to full alert.

"What'll it be?"

His gaze clung to the way her dark hair, longer than he remembered, spilled over her shoulders. She wore a gauzy white tunic with a lacy camisole underneath and faded blue jeans that encased her long legs like a well-worn glove.

"Sir? Is everything okay?"

Justin was brought from his trance by the new bartender's insistence. "I'm sorry, yeah, what craft beers do you have?"

"Got Zeke, if you like pale. Good hop. A couple of the darker beers. And an Irish stout we call Eventide, if you prefer a malt."

"I'll try the Eventide, thanks." Justin fumbled in his wallet as he kept one eye on Georgia seated behind the desk, engaged in a phone conversation that appeared to be challenging. She cradled her forehead in her palm as she shook her head. Maybe it was a problem at home. Maybe with her husband.

He fished for a ten and laid the money on the counter just as she finished her conversation. His gaze lingered on the soft alabaster curve of her throat as she leaned her head back and stretched her arms over her head. The young woman he'd fallen in love with back in high school had been replaced by a woman even more beautiful than the last time he saw her.

"Here you go, man. Let me know what you think," the bartender said.

"Thanks." Justin took the beer. He glanced up and across the space separating him from Georgia and met her gaze. His grip tightened on the glass, fearful he might drop it. He should just walk back there and say hello. It'd be the decent thing to do.

She lifted her hand and waved him over, giving him that smile that had tormented his dreams on more than one occasion.

Chapter Three

GEORGIA GRIPPED THE ARM OF her father's ancient desk chair as she waited for Justin Reed to step through that door. More than a few years had passed since she'd seen him last and their parting hadn't been pleasant. She'd met his gaze across the bar—distance and shadows playing havoc with her vision, making it impossible to discern his features. Was he balding like so many men his age? Had he put on a few pounds? She glanced at the dark computer screen and pinched her cheeks, hoping for the best but knowing she often wore the bags of exhausted motherhood beneath her eyes these days.

"Hey, Georgia." Justin stepped inside the door, a beer in his hand. Much to her dismay, he'd aged to perfection. Broad shoulders in a smoky gray T-shirt made his blue eyes smolder and emphasized the muscular outline of a fit body and slender waist. She dared not venture any further down, too easily remembering the bliss she'd experienced as she'd wrapped herself around him.

"Hey," she forced out through the rapid tattoo of her heart. Her fingers tingled with the memory of his flesh against hers. It had been a long time since she'd been with a man—longer still with the man to whom she'd first given her heart and soul. "I wasn't sure you'd make it with all your teacher responsibilities."

He smiled, quickly ducking his head to conceal a bashful grin. The dimple she remembered on his left cheek was now covered by a soft, light brown beard, shaved close enough to send gooseflesh to rise where it would leave a sensational burn on her sensitive skin.

"Yeah, well, school's out for summer, as the old song goes." His gaze rose to hers. Heat sparkled in those blue orbs. She didn't need to ask to know his thoughts had traveled the same route as hers to that long and very hot—in more ways than one—summer that they'd spent together. Georgia cleared her throat.

"I see the committee is out there waiting on us. Probably don't need to give them something to talk about, huh?" She rose from the desk. He stood aside, waiting for her to walk ahead. "Thank you, sir," she said, edging past him with a quick smile.

"Georgie," he said quietly.

The nickname stopped her in her tracks. They stood toe-to-toe in the doorway. Barely a breath could pass between them. His gaze lingered on hers a moment longer.

"It's good to see you," he said finally.

She held his eyes, watching his face lower to hers. Grabbing what wits she had left, she scooted through the door. "We'd better get this meeting started. I've got work to do."

She purposely distanced herself, taking a chair across the table from Justin. Seated on the other side of Jolie, Georgia tried to keep her focus on her notes and ignore Jolie's overt attempts to flirt with Justin, trying to do the same with his darted looks to come to his rescue. The group quickly covered what Langley's would bring in terms of equipment and staff, and when they would need access to the building to set up before the reception.

Georgia noted that the more Jolie drank, the looser her tongue became—and so, too, any inhibitions the woman might have possessed. Jolie had removed her summer cardigan that she'd worn over a very revealing skimpy sundress, then dropped her arm over the back of Justin's chair, now and again rubbing his shoulder.

"You know what, I have a confession to make," she said with squeaky giggle.

"Maybe that you've had one too many appletinis tonight?" Maddie interjected. As president of the senior class, she'd run a tight ship. Presently, however, Jolie gave new meaning to the term 'tight'.

In true high-school fashion, Jolie stuck her tongue out at her classmate, then giggled again. She looked from Jake to Justin and a wicked smile parted her red lips. "You boys remember the Friday night potlucks we used to have in the neighborhood during the summers?"

Justin glanced at Jake, who had leaned back in his chair, nursing his bourbon and water. His gaze was on the woman who held everyone's attention.

Jake grinned. "We did have some good times, as I remember."

Georgia closed her notebook and prepared to leave. The whole situation seemed surreal. She'd gotten over the wildfire of rumors that had circulated for a time about her and Jake. They'd stung, but she was tough. Honed by fire, her aunt had told her when she'd slip into self-pity. She knew the truth of what had happened that night and that was all that mattered. She glanced at Justin, wondering if he'd even been aware of the rumors. Jolie's next words stopped her train of thought.

"There was a whole lot of hankie-pankie going on at some of those parties, as I recall." She leaned forward and gave Jake a wink. "Course, back then you weren't married." She nudged Justin's arm. "Neither were you. But I was never very good at getting your attention back then, was I?" She traced her finger along the edge of his collar.

Justin's eyes met Georgia's.

"But I did manage to get your brother's." She sat back then and pouted her pretty red mouth. "I wanted you both. Just for comparison's sake, of course. And poo on you, Justin Reed, you just couldn't be bothered."

Mac choked on his beer. Maddie stared slack-jawed at Jolie.

Jolie shrugged. "What girl doesn't fantasize about a ménage at least once?"

"Okay, that's it for tonight." Maddie stood. "Enough treks down fantasy lane." She directed her look at Georgia. "We'll have the Trolley Barn open by three o'clock for you and your team." Maddie slammed her folder shut. "Meeting adjourned."

"Hey, why don't we head back to my place for a nightcap?" Jake suggested. "Faith had a party tonight. I'm sure there are some great leftovers."

Jolie attempted to stand, grabbing Justin's arm as she teetered on her spike-heeled sandals. "Oh, dear, I think I'm going to need a ride." She leaned her chin on Justin's shoulder.

He glanced at Mac. "You're the only one besides me and Maddie who should even be behind a wheel. You do the honors," Justin said, prying Jolie's hand from his arm. "I have something I need to do."

Jolie frowned.

Mac, on the other hand—divorced once and with no prospects on the horizon—dove at the opportunity to play the white knight. Everyone except Jolie, it appeared, knew how Mac had carried a torch for her since high school.

"Absolutely," he said, and skirted around the table to grab Jolie's sweater. He held out his elbow. "Your chariot awaits, m'lady."

Stumbling as she walked past, Jolie stopped and put her hand on Georgia's arm. "How is that precious little boy of yours?"

Kolby was not a topic Georgia chose to discuss in public, and certainly not with a classmate who hadn't proven her trustworthiness—sober or not.

"He's fine, thank you for asking," she answered firmly.

Jolie seemed to want to belabor Georgia's discomfiture. "What is he now, about three or four? It must be hard doing what you do as a single mom. I mean, running a business and all—your clients surely keep you busy night after night."

It was a veiled slap in the face and Georgia straightened her shoulders, battling the desire to knock Ms. Jolie on her bony little ass.

"Take her home, Mac," Justin ordered, steering Jolie towards the door and all but sticking his boot in her backside.

"Sorry, Georgia," Maddie said, shaking her head. "Some people never seem to make it past high school emotionally."

Jake hung back and smiled as he placed his arm around Justin. "Jolie really likes you, man." He punched his shoulder. "You sure you don't want to take her home yourself?"

Justin narrowed his gaze on his brother. "What about that woman makes you think I'd have any interest? Jesus, Jake, she needs help."

Jake shrugged. "Just trying to get you to have a little fun while you're here."

"Yeah, well, don't," Justin warned.

Georgia kept her gaze to the floor as Jake walked by. The

rumors that she'd slept with him had spread like wildfire just after the incident at the bar. It had been twice that a Reed male had humiliated her, never refuting the gossip, never showing any gratitude for the kindness she'd shown. But what would be the point of dredging up the past? They all had moved on with their lives.

"Good to see you, Justin," she said and managed to skim past his outstretched hand as he tried to stop her. She hurried back to the office and shut the door. What had she been thinking? Had she thought that she could easily dismiss her emotions? That she'd feel nothing at seeing him? She survived losing him once—had even learned to love again, only to have that, too, snatched away. But she had Kolby and he was the only man she needed in her life.

A knock sounded on the door before Justin gently opened it and stuck his head in. "Tank warned me that he has his eye on me. Should I be concerned?"

Georgia's best-laid plans to not get involved with Justin Reed sputtered like air from a balloon. She brushed her hair back. "Come on in. It seems we have some things we need to talk about."

He stepped in and shut the door.

"I've only got sweet tea." She led him into the small apartment. She now lived with her aunt who helped with Kolby's specific needs, but she'd kept the apartment as a sanctuary when she needed time to rejuvenate. "How have you been?" she asked, pouring his tea.

"Okay. Good." He stood at the entrance, uncertain whether to come in. "You?"

"Come on in." She handed him a glass of tea and ushered him to the couch. She chose a chair across from him. After an awkward minute or two, she tried to cut some of the tension she felt. "So, almost ten years. Pretty amazing. You married?"

He held his glass between his hands, not looking up. He shook his head, then sighed. "Listen." He looked up and she was caught in his gaze. "I don't have any right to ask this, but I'm curious." The corner of his mouth lifted in a pensive smile.

Georgia steeled herself. She had a pretty good idea what he was about to ask.

"I was wondering about you and Jake."

So, he *had* heard. She met his steady gaze. "Me and Jake?" She feigned ignorance about what he was talking about.

He raised his brows. "I heard after I left that things got friendly between the two of you. Which I found odd since you told me last time we were together that my father tried to keep you from me. Apparently, it didn't count with my brother."

Georgia shook her head. "Don't be an ass, Justin." She looked away and sighed. "Besides, what do you care? You were up north with that friend of yours, Leslie somebody."

"Reverend Cook," he corrected her.

"Yeah, well, pastors have needs too, so I understand."

He stood and held out his glass. "You have anything stronger than tea?"

"I do, but neither of us is going to drink anything stronger than tea. I remember what happened last time." She held up her glass. "Tea only."

"Fine." He sat down and draped his arm over the back of the couch. "For the record, Leslie and I dated a total of once, back in college. It bombed and we chose to stay friends."

She waved his comment away. "That's none of my business."

"Like what happened between you and Jake is none of mine, you mean?" He shrugged. "Not that I blame you, of course. He can be as charming as a snake."

That hit hard. Harder than she'd anticipated. He'd apparently bought into the rumors and like everyone else had, believing that the rebellious girl she once was hadn't changed since high school. "Okay, I'm only going to say this once, and then you have to promise me you'll leave."

A flicker of hesitancy passed through his blue eyes, but then he nodded.

"And for the record"—she used his phrase—"you walked out on me. We weren't dating then, we aren't dating now. But out of respect for the friendship we had, I will share this once."

He looked at his shoe. "Okay, fair enough."

For reasons, she dared not toy with, he seemed to need an explanation. To speculate why was to play with fire. "Okay, I was working my shift when Mac and your brother came in with a few of the guys. They were making the rounds for his bachelor party, and we were the last stop."

Justin leaned back. He seemed to be listening, but his gaze was where his boot crossed over his knee. Cowboy boots were new but not out of place on him. He'd always possessed the qualities of a true cowboy in addition to his deep love of horses—he invoked the qualities of honesty, hard work, and kindness that she'd long admired and loved about him.

"They'd been drinking and the beer and bourbon had been flowing pretty freely. Jake came over to talk with me at the bar. He'd had a few so I listened and he felt the need to explain the grievous mistake he'd made in telling your dad about us. He told me he felt bad that he'd been the cause of our break-up."

Justin swiped his hand over his mouth, tossed her a quick glance, and sighed.

In a strange way, Georgia now understood why Justin

needed to hear this from her. They'd been in love once. This was his brother. The rumors must have been as painful for him as they'd been for her. She needed to clear the air, so that they could get on with their lives.

"At the time, I had just lost someone very special to me and I suppose I was vulnerable. Maybe I wasn't thinking clearly, I don't know." She wanted to move to his side, take his hand, but she dared not make such a move. Not knowing his reaction, it was best to keep things platonic. "Jake and I were talking. He was actually telling me what was going on with you. How much you loved Montana, like your mom. How you used to love the fishing trips with your uncle and he how much he hated the outdoors."

Justin's brow furrowed and he looked at her, holding her gaze. "The next thing we knew, his friends had left him. Maybe it was a prank." She shrugged. "Maybe they thought he was going to get lucky."

Justin looked away.

"I took his keys and offered to drive him home. He didn't want Faith to see him like that. So, I took him instead to the little motel that used to be down the road. While I was helping him inside, he got sick. I got him out of his shirt so it wouldn't stain the bedspread. While I was rinsing it in the bathroom, he fell onto the bed and passed out cold."

Justin shook his head.

"I laid the shirt over the chair to dry, locked him and his keys in the room, and walked back to the bar to finish my shift." She stopped long enough to gauge Justin's reaction. Though in all probability, it didn't seem to matter in the big picture of things. He had his life in Montana. Her life was here with her son and what was left of her family. "To be honest, this is the first time I've seen Jake since that night." She shrugged. "For all I know, he doesn't even remember how he got to the hotel."

"He must have known, Georgia. It was Mac who told me about it at Jake's wedding."

"Wow, okay, you've known this since the wedding? Well, I imagine Mac's story was far more exciting, right?" She stood and walked to the door that led to the back of the lot. Opening the screen, she walked out and stood on the small porch. She sensed him standing at the door, staring at her. "You know," she said, "if it had concerned you so much, you could have picked up the phone, or sent me an email."

"That didn't seem to work too well for me last time," he said.

Burn. She looked over her shoulder. "You could have tried."

Silence stretched between them.

"You have a child?" he asked.

The question was out of the blue. Unexpected.

"It's none of your concern, Justin." She turned and opened the door. "If you'll please leave, I have a lot to do. I do hope this helps you to move on."

He stepped outside and looked at her, seeming to study her face. She looked into those clear blue eyes, remembering the look of adoration she'd once seen in them. A different place. A different time.

He gave her a pensive smile. "Yeah, looks like we've both moved on." He leaned forward and placed his lips on her forehead as he'd often done when they'd dated. It was a comforting gesture to her. Tears pricked at the backs of her eyes.

He walked across the gravel lot, disappearing around the corner. With his departure came a renewed sense of loss.

JUSTIN ARRIVED HOME TO FIND the French doors to the patio open and his brother sitting alone in the dark. He had a drink in his hand.

"How'd it go with Georgia?" he asked, not turning around.

Justin sat down opposite Jake. He glanced at the glass as Jake swirled the ice.

"It's water, in case you're wondering," he said, as though answering Justin's silent concern.

"We managed to get a few things cleared up," Justin said.

"Yeah? You mean like the rumors that Mac started after my bachelor party?"

Justin straightened. "Wait. You knew about that?" Justin leaned forward and peered at his brother. All this time he knew and never thought to refute it? At the very least, mention the fact?

"Yes, but until this moment, I hadn't realized that *you'd* heard anything. Mac was the only person I spoke to about this—him and Faith. And Faith isn't the type to spread rumors." Jake's steady gaze held Justin's. "Nothing happened that night, I swear. Georgia saved me from an embarrassing situation all around."

Justin shook his head. So much time wasted. "I don't know if you realize it or not, but those rumors came back to Georgia. They hurt her reputation, her pride. She didn't deserve that."

"I don't know what Mac was thinking," they said simultaneously.

Justin looked at his brother. It was the first time in ages that it felt like they were on the same page.

"I had no idea the rumor had gotten back to Georgia. I'm going to give Mac a piece of my mind," Jake said.

"I'd like to give him a piece of my fist," Justin remarked.

Jake was quiet a moment, then spoke. "Listen, clearly there's been a lot of misunderstanding going on. First, let's get something straight. We're talking Mac. The guy's been though a nightmare of a divorce—which doesn't excuse anything, I admit." He held up his hand. "I swear, I think he likes to make up stuff just to create some excitement in his life. Did you see how he jumped at the chance to take Jolie home?"

Justin nodded, though it didn't lessen his annoyance with Mac "Yeah, now there's just one more thing I need to get cleared up." As long as they were getting things out in the open, Justin decided to lay it all out to his brother. "Explain telling Dad about me and Georgia," Justin asked.

Jake lowered his head, then met Justin's gaze "That's not a time in my life I'm proud of. It's true, I went to Dad and told him about you two, when you told me that you were thinking of not going to college because you thought she might be pregnant. It was a selfish thing to do, I admit. I was jealous. But I didn't want to see you give up your future that way."

"That was my choice to make, Jake."

Jake sighed and looked away. "I know, I know. And I did apologize to Georgia that night of my bachelor party. That's the only reason I went over to talk to her. She told me then that she'd told you the same thing. That she wouldn't be able to live with herself if you'd given up going to college for her. Mac and the guys perceived my talking to her as something else entirely. Mac just put two and two together and created a story."

The bitterness that had taken root inside him began to weaken in light of the truth.

"I'm guessing you confronted her about this rumor business tonight and it didn't go over well. Am I right?"

Jake asked.

All of the frustration he'd been carrying around for so long came out in a heavy sigh. He nodded. "She was pissed. After she told me what happened, she asked me to leave." He hung his head, clasping his hands over his knees. "I was angry with everyone after the funeral."

"Angry with Georgia?" Jake asked. "I had a feeling that you'd taken off after the service to follow her. I saw her too, that day."

"I'm afraid, yeah, that I screwed that up then. And I may have done the same again tonight." Justin raked a hand through his hair and leaned back, looking up at the night sky. Things seemed so much simpler back on his ranch. He blew out another sigh and sat up. "What do you know about this son that Jolie was asking about?"

Jake shrugged. "I heard at one time that she'd been involved with a guy a few years back—country singer that was playing at her dad's bar. I don't know much more than that. Maybe you should ask her."

"Yeah," Justin said. "Except I'm pretty sure if I step within ten feet of the bar, Tank will have my head on a platter."

Jake shrugged. "Seems to me you've been sitting up there in nowhere land stewing about this woman for a damn long time. You've been too stubborn to admit that you still have feelings for her."

Justin looked at his brother. "I've been such a jerk. I'm sorry I didn't ask you about this sooner, instead of taking Mac's word."

"Yeah, Mac can be a pain at times, but don't be too hard on the guy. He's been through enough crap, too. The guy's last divorce was ugly. I mean, *really* ugly," Jake said.

"I can't believe how much energy I've wasted being bitter over this."

Jake grinned. "You do tend to have a few asshole-type tendencies."

"And…*we are* twins." Justin smiled in return. "Maybe we should get Mac signed up with some kind of dating service or something."

Jake's unbridled laughter lifted Justin's heart. It felt right to have things settled between them again.

"Little brother—and I say that because technically, I came first—you have a much bigger issue than Mac to deal with. There's a lady out there who you'd have lassoed the moon for at one time. If you still feel something for her, you need to do something about it. Let her know."

"And why all of a sudden are you being so supportive of my possibly having any relationship with Georgia Langley?" Justin narrowed his gaze on his brother.

"Because, I realize what an ass I'd been back then—"

"Back then?" Justin grinned and Jake flipped him the finger.

"I was jealous of what you two had. It was that simple. And I knew that it wouldn't take much to plant a seed of doubt in Dad's head about how it would appear to the community and to his beloved social circles if his son was dating the rebellious daughter of a honkytonk bar's owner."

"You were jealous of me?" Justin chuckled. His brother had always been first in everything—sports, girls, grades—and especially in business sense.

"It was high school. Few of us get through without being an ass at least fifty percent of the time." Jake stood then and held out his arms. "Come here, you jerk." He pulled Justin into a warm embrace and slapped him on the back.

"Hey." Jake stepped back. "Are you going to go golfing with us in the morning? A few of the guys are meeting over at the club."

Justin followed his brother into the house, waiting as he locked up and set the alarm system. "I'm not much of a golfer. A club might slip and bean Mac on the head." He grinned. "Besides, I've got some stuff I need to do."

Jake chuckled "It might happen, anyway. Okay." He shrugged. "Good luck with that *stuff* you have to do."

༒

JUSTIN WOKE AT THE SOUND of the alarm he'd set for five thirty. He pulled on his old T-shirt and a pair of sweats that he usually wore for runs before school. He'd laid awake a good part of the night thinking about Georgia, about how he'd screwed things up and what he could possibly do to make them right—or whether she'd even give him a chance to do so. It was, he had to consider, possible that she wanted nothing more to do with him. But when he'd looked into her eyes, he thought he saw something—a spark of interest. He'd definitely felt something. Maybe he was delusional, but he thought she felt it, too.

The slap of his tennis shoes in the early-morning silence of the gated community filled him with a sense of nostalgia. Back in school, he used to get up early and run before school—sometimes with Jake, most days alone. He found that he enjoyed the solitude, the ability to think about things. It was no surprise, then, that the great outdoors of Montana would appeal to him.

"Well, hey there, stranger."

Justin glanced to his side and spied Jolie's smiling face as she slowed her red BMW convertible to keep pace with him. He was mildly surprised that she'd be awake at this hour. "Morning, Jolie."

He continued, keeping his stride slow and steady, secretly hoping she might get bored and get on with her day. "You're up early," he commented, keeping his eyes on the road ahead.

"Oh, I needed to run out early and pick up my dress at the dry cleaners before I head to my day at the spa. I just can't believe that this reunion is finally going to happen."

"Doesn't hardly seem like that long, does it?" He kept the conversation short as benign as possible.

"You know, it almost didn't happen at all. Maddie was pregnant *again* at the time of our five-year reunion."

"Is that right?" In all fairness, he hadn't been paying attention. Once he'd gotten his mom settled in eastern Montana a few short months after his Dad's funeral, he'd put everyone and everything in Atlanta out of his mind. Everyone…except Georgia.

"Well, it's absolutely true that if I hadn't lit a fire under our illustrious class officers we might have had to wait until…God knows when!" She drove a moment in silence. "Actually, I think that it's all worked out perfectly, if I do say so myself."

"Well, I'd say our class is lucky to have you living right here so you can keep everyone in line." He glanced at her and she responded with a beaming grin.

"Why, thank you kindly, sir. At least there's one person who sees my worth." She chuckled. "You know, though, in all my planning I did manage to forget one tiny little detail. I was hoping *you* might be able to help me with that."

Justin felt his phone vibrate in his pocket. Any other day, he'd probably ignore it. His gut cautioned it might save his life just now. "Excuse me, Jolie. I need to get this." He tapped his phone and grinned, seeing who it was. This might be a very good sign. He cleared his throat, turned on his heel, and jogged off in the other direction. "See you tomorrow night," he called over his shoulder as he pressed the callback number and silently thanked his lucky stars.

"Hey, sorry, I was out for a run. Couldn't get to my phone fast enough." He stopped at the corner of the block and rested against a tall brick wall surrounding one of the stately homes that were once considered the mansions of Buckhead.

"I was hoping that I hadn't woken you." Georgia's voice was soft, a little groggy still, as though she'd picked up the phone and called him just after waking. He pictured her sitting up in bed, her covers tucked around her, her hair mussed from sleeping…her silky skin still warm.

He turned and leaned against the wall and exerted some of his pent-up sexual energy by doing a few one-armed push-ups. The activity, he realized, wasn't doing much to ease his libido.

"Listen, I felt badly about how we left things last night. Any chance we could meet for a cup of coffee and talk some more?"

"I'm glad you called," he said and straightened. *So glad*. "I'd like that. Let me pick you up. What's your address?"

"How'd you know I wasn't living in the old house?" she asked. There was a smile in her voice.

Busted.

"I happened to be in the neighborhood." It was a sloppy lie.

If she noticed, she didn't point it out. "I just couldn't stay there," she said quietly. "It needed too much renovation and there wasn't enough room for us at the apartment. Besides, I grew up in that bar. I didn't want that for my son."

"Right." The son she'd expressly told him was none of his business.

"So, where are you living?" he asked, curious to know why she seemed guarded on the subject of her son.

"With my aunt. It's over a block from the old place—a big yellow three-story clapboard." She hesitated. "Are you sure you don't mind?"

"It'll be great to have some time with you, Georgie." He automatically used the pet name he'd given her when they were dating. "I need a shower. How about I pick you up in an hour?"

"Sounds good," she said.

"Does to me, too," he responded. "See you soon."

Fifteen minutes later he was whistling in the shower. Good lord, he hadn't felt this good in months. Things had gotten cleared up between him and Jake, though his brother still had some drinking issues that concerned Justin. And now, fate had provided him with a chance to make things right between him and Georgia. He'd lost her once. He wasn't about to let her slip through his fingers again.

Rejuvenated, Justin set to the task of rummaging through the refrigerator to put together a picnic lunch. He had a very special place in mind to take Georgia.

"Goodness, look at you." Faith dropped her tote on the floor and leaned against the kitchen island, its surface spread with an array of veggies, cheeses, and condiments for making sandwiches. "Looks like you're either very hungry, or you're planning a"—she looked at him—"picnic?" She eyed him. "Does this have to do with Jolie?"

Justin darted a look at her. "Hell, no. I mean, no, it doesn't. I'm meeting an old friend for coffee."

"Would that be Georgia?" she asked with a knowing smile.

"Good to know my brother does communicate on occasion." He glanced at her as he continued making the sandwiches.

She raised a brow.

"Yes, as a matter of fact. Georgia and I dated once way back in high school." He brushed the information aside, hoping not to get into why they'd broken up. "By the way, do you have a thermos?"

Faith grinned. "I do, and an insulated basket you can put those in." She proceeded to help by making coffee and filling the thermos. She added a small bag of cookies to the lunch. "I have to say, Justin, this Georgia is one lucky girl." A sad smile crossed her lips. "I can't remember the last time Jake did something so romantic."

Justin chuckled. "Not sure it's going to make a difference. Our track record isn't exemplary."

Faith studied him. "Well, I believe in second chances." She leaned over and kissed his cheek. "Maybe I'll surprise Jake at work with a picnic lunch today."

A few moments later, he dropped the basket in the back of the cab and climbed in behind the wheel. Admonishing himself mentally for doing so, he checked for the ancient condom he carried in his wallet. "You're getting way ahead of yourself," he muttered, stuffing the billfold in his back pocket.

It didn't take long to spot the house. It stood out among the others with its mustard yellow color and white trim. It sat at the edge of the Inman Park district, one of Atlanta's first suburbs built primarily for those who owned businesses downtown. The neighborhood was now an eclectic blend of Victorian and modern housing, one-story bungalows bumping up to the yards of some of the grand old homes complete with gingerbread trim and wrap-around porches.

He swallowed, surprised by what felt like first date jitters as he walked up to the front door. Delicate white lace curtains adorned the tall windows. A grouping of white wicker furniture sat clustered at one end of the porch, making an inviting gathering place to visit on a summer night. Scattered across an old braided rug was a plastic *Hot Wheels* track and a handful of cars left by their owner after play.

He knocked twice before the door opened and a little boy—his head wrapped with a red bandana, and one eye covered with a patch—stood staring up at him. The patch didn't impede the thick-lensed glasses he wore.

"You must be Kolby?" Justin held out his hand in greeting.

"Who wants to know?" the boy asked with a rasp in his bird-like voice.

"Kolby." Georgia appeared at the door. "That's no way to speak to someone you're meeting." She clamped her hands down over his bony little shoulders. "Kolby, this is an old friend of mine, Justin Reed. We used to be classmates in school."

Kolby gave him a once over, lingering on his boots. "Are you a cowboy?"

Justin grinned. "Not like John Wayne, but I do have horses on my ranch. Does that count?"

The boy tipped his head and shrugged. "Kinda, I guess." He tentatively accepted Justin's hand and gave it a quick shake. "Are you taking my mom out on a date?"

"Kolby," Georgia admonished. "We're just going for coffee."

The young boy frowned, giving his mom a puzzled look. "But you were a long time getting ready. Jeez, you're even wearing that fancy perfume that Aunt Mae and I got you for your birthday."

Georgia's cheeks blushed a pretty shade of pink. She offered Justin an embarrassed look.

"You do look great," he said. Her simple sundress topped with a faded jean jacket and those flirty cowboy boots made his Montana heart flutter.

She picked up the little boy amid squeals and giggles, squeezing him until he pleaded to be let go.

"I'm not a baby anymore, Mom." He skirted around her and went straight to the woman who stood at the kitchen door, a dishtowel in her hands. She reached out and patted his shoulder.

"You behave yourself, young man, and don't go talking to your mama that way or there'll be no bedtime story for you tonight." The woman with silvery long hair braided to one side nodded, acknowledging Justin. "I'm Georgia's aunt. Her Daddy was my brother."

"I'm sorry for your loss, ma'am. It's good that Georgia and Kolby have the love and support of family." Justin met her steady gaze, fairly certain she was assessing his worth. She cocked her head and gave Georgia a quiet smile.

"You ready?" he asked Georgia. "I've got my truck outside." He stepped aside so she could walk ahead of him and caught the look of concern in Aunt Mae's parting glance. "I'll be careful," he said with a smile.

"See that you are, Mr. Reed," she said firmly.

Once on the road, he headed in the direction of the equine ranch he'd once worked at on weekends. It was not far from the spot back in the woods where high school kids used to meet for bonfires and parties. It's where they'd first met. He hoped she'd remember the place. "Hey, do you know if the old Stoneville place is still standing?" His heart tilted at the sound of her laughter.

"I haven't heard about that place in years. I would guess it's been torn down to make room for all the developments going on out this way," she said.

"What do you say we find out?" He grinned and turned

down a familiar road that twisted through a forest of trees. "Didn't this used to be an old dirt road?"

"Welcome to progress," Georgia said, her gaze on a number of larger homes built far off the main road, purposely camouflaged, it appeared, by the trees.

They followed another curve or two where the asphalt came to an abrupt stop, turning to gravel. Deep ruts threaded the road where four-wheelers and trucks had driven through the mud and rock. A "no passing" sign hung lopsided on a post listing precariously to one side. "Does this look familiar?" he asked.

She sat forward, peering through the window. Tall Georgia pine and ancient oaks surrounded them. Pine straw blanketed most of the ground. At the edge of the road stood a dogwood tree in bloom, its fragrant flowers adding splendor to the woods. Georgia shook her head. "It doesn't, no. But it's beautiful, wherever we are." She glanced at him with a smile, then quickly looked away.

"From the look of that busted chain, it appears somebody was checking out something back in those woods." He glanced at her and grinned. "You game?"

"If you are." She shrugged, followed by a soft laugh.

That was the Georgia he'd fallen in love with. Fearless, ready for adventure. He eased around the post and drove over the chain half-buried in the mud. The truck jostled over the ruts, and though she braced one hand above her head for balance, her laughter prompted memories of carefree days when they'd taken his old truck out mudding.

"Hey, look there." He slowed the truck at the sight of an old picnic table, one seat missing and turned on its side. Not far off were remnants of an old weed-covered stone ring. "I think that's our fire pit." He stopped the truck and got out to investigate the site. He scanned the area, now thick with underbrush, and thought of wild animals—something that had never occurred to them in high school.

Georgia sat watching from the truck.

"Aren't you curious to see what we might find out here?" he called over his shoulder.

She hopped down from the truck and walked cautiously through the weeds. "Someone's lost virginity?" She tossed him a grin.

He nodded with a chuckle. "I think I can manage to clean this out and build us a fire."

"You think that will stave off the axe-murderers and zombies?"

He began to pull the overgrowth from the stones. "There is a blanket and picnic basket in the truck."

"Well, aren't you the well-prepared boy scout?" she teased as she scanned the area.

He glanced up, her smile hitting him with a sucker punch to his gut. "Ready, maybe." He grinned. "Not so sure about the boy scout part, though."

She raised a brow, turned on her boot heel, and walked back to the truck. He watched the hem of her dress flip with each step. He tore his gaze from her long, bare legs, tamping down his lust. He wasn't sure where this day was headed, but he sure as hell knew he didn't want it to end.

They spread the blanket on an old log and shared the lunch he'd packed, followed by steaming mugs of coffee and Faith's chocolate chip cookies. The sky had gone from misty filtered sun to a muted gray, signaling the possibility of a stray shower.

"I'm impressed, Mr. Reed. I don't think I've ever had a man cook for me before," she said, peering at him over the rim of her coffee cup.

"I question whether lunchmeat sandwiches constitute

'cooking', but I can't take all the credit. My sister-in-law, Faith, offered her help—and the cookies." He held up his dessert.

"Faith," Georgia repeated. "That's a pretty name." She crossed her boots at the ankle, holding her cup in both hands. "I guess there *has* been one little man who's cooked for me…well"—she laughed— "attempted to cook for me." She gave him a side look. "Kolby once tried to make me breakfast." She smiled at her secret thoughts, then glanced at him. "Let's just say he could use some more training before he opens his first restaurant."

Justin studied her. "I'd like to know more about him. He seems like a great kid." He hoped she'd open up about her son.

"Hey," she said, straightening suddenly. "Do you think the old Stoneville house is still around here?"

Chapter Four

GEORGIA AVOIDED HIS GAZE, SEEING the curiosity that flashed across his face. She was grateful when he helped gather their picnic items instead of pursuing the subject of her son.

She waited behind as he dropped the basket in the truck and locked it. He tucked the blanket under his arm. "You know, I haven't been back here since the night we met," she said as he returned to her. His blue-eyed gaze met hers and the memory of that night—a lifetime ago—played in her brain, including the first time he'd kissed her. "Now that I'm all grown up, it might not seem so spooky."

He took her hand. "Come on, then. Let's check it out."

She followed as he led the way through the woods, spotting relics—beer cans, an old shoe, a crumpled cigarette pack—scattered along the way.

"Chances are we're headed in the right direction." Justin grinned over his shoulder.

Between the clouds gathering overhead and the dense forest of trees, Georgia didn't lag far behind.

"I think I see it," he said, pushing aside a spray of low pine branches.

She followed him into a clearing and stood at his shoulder as they stared at the ramshackle bones of what was once a fine rural home.

"I thought this place was on the register of historic homes," she said, glancing at him. "Wasn't it supposedly used as a hospital during the Civil War?"

The majority of windows on the main floor were boarded up. The upper story windows stared cold and dark out over the trees.

"That's what I understood." He shrugged. "I'll go around to the other side. You stay here. Hold this." He handed her the blanket and eyed the front porch roof. A corner drooped precariously low on one side. "Whatever you do, don't go near that porch."

He trotted off.

"This isn't much good against a zombie attack," she called after him as he disappeared around the corner of the house.

She scanned her surroundings, her senses heightened to the strange woodland sounds. A rumble of thunder rolled across the sky, followed by a loud bang. Her heart leapt. Twice more the banging came, and her heart tried to claw its way out her chest. More disturbing was the silence that followed. It had seemed an eternity since Justin had walked around to the other side of the house. She chided herself mentally for letting her imagination spin into overdrive.

A single raindrop landed on her arm, followed by another, then another. She glanced up as the sky seemed to open up. A torrential rain fell in straight sheets from the heavens. "Justin!" She blinked away the temporary obstacle of water obscuring her vision.

"Come on, follow me."

She felt his hand grab hers, tugging her around to the side of the house as they ran through the torrential rain.

"Down here." He pointed to the open cellar door.

"You're serious?" The entrance yawned like a dark cave.

"It's pitch black down there," she reasoned, even as her sodden dress began to cling to her body.

"We could try to run back through the woods to the truck." The grin on his rain-streaked face made her smile.

"Why is it every time I'm with you I find myself in trouble?"

"You used to like trouble," he said with a wicked smile.

"You first." She cocked her head and stepped aside.

He rolled his eyes and side-stepped his way down the five or six narrow stone steps. At the bottom, he held up his hand to guide her down.

Out of the rain, at least, her eyes adjusted to the dank, dirt-floored basement. An overwhelming stench of decay—she didn't want to think about *what*—brought bile to her throat.

"There's some steps over there." Justin brushed his hand through his short hair, causing it to go every which way.

Messy, a little reckless—the thought of how they'd once been stirred in her blood.

"Watch your step," he said, switching on the flashlight on his cell phone.

"For dead bodies, you mean," she muttered, stepping gingerly around shadowy objects she'd just as soon not identify.

Sodden, she clung to the blanket beneath her jacket and gripped the railing with the other hand. She followed his light up the rickety wood steps, praying with every creak that the step wouldn't collapse. They emerged from the bowels of the house into the kitchen. Shivering, she wrapped her arms around her and realized she'd left her phone and purse in the backseat of his truck.

"I'm looking for some light. My phone's about to die," he said as he rummaged through the cupboards.

Her teeth began to chatter. "Is it c-c-cold in here?"

He walked over and held her shoulders. "Where's the blanket?"

She pulled it from under her jean jacket, where she'd tucked it away as they ran.

"Take off your jacket and dress, and wrap it around you." He opened the blanket with a quick snap and held it out.

She opened her mouth to argue.

"It's not like I haven't seen you, Georgie. Come on, you'll catch your death." He chuckled. "Fine. I'll look away."

Georgia quickly removed her jacket and dress, laying them to dry over a kitchen chair. She stepped into the blanket as he wrapped it around her. He turned her to face him, his grip still on the blanket.

"That should help some."

She met his gaze and held it as he lowered his mouth to hers. She gave in to the moment, relishing the taste of him, the way he coaxed her patiently until she deepened the kiss. She placed her hand on his wet shirt and withdrew from his grasp.

"What about you?" she asked.

He grinned. "You want me to take off my clothes?"

She glanced at the floor. "I could see that being problematic." She searched his eyes. "Maybe we should see if the fireplace still works."

He nodded.

She wandered down the narrow corridor to what would have been the sitting room or parlor at one time. Indeed, there was a stone fireplace, but half the face had fallen into a state of disrepair, making it impossible to use.

Georgia sensed him standing behind her.

"That night was one of the best times of my life," he said. The soft tone in his voice sent chills over her bare flesh. She hugged the blanket closer and looked over her shoulder to see him rummaging through a pile of objects left by trespassers and previous owners.

"Some of this stuff is pretty old." She tried to change the subject. "You'd think someone would have seen its value," Georgia said, running her fingers over the dusty, curved back of an ornate sitting chair.

Justin picked through a stack of old books, peering behind a crate. "Sometimes, people don't see the value of what they left behind until it's too late."

She pondered the double meaning and wondered if he realized the wisdom of his words.

"Bingo." He lifted up an old lantern from behind a crate. "Now, if it has any oil left in it." He rifled through his pockets, pulling out a book of matches with the *Langley's* logo on the front. "Glad I happened to pick these up the other night." He lit the wick. The tiny flame flickered bravely, offering at least an imaginary warmth.

A loud thump from upstairs captured Georgia's attention. She darted a look at Justin, who appeared equally as startled. She wanted to wipe off his wicked grin. He waggled his brows.

"That's not funny," she whispered, moving next to him. He placed an arm around her and, holding the lantern high, guided her to the base of the stairwell.

"I'll go check it out," he said. Justin patted her shoulder and headed up the steps.

Hastily, she followed, grabbing the waistband of his jeans. He glanced back at her and grinned.

"I've seen those movies. No way in hell am I staying down here alone."

He made a ghost-like sound and she batted his backside with her hand, receiving a soft chuckle in return.

Reaching the top of the stairs, she realized gratefully that the light was better where the windows weren't impeded by boards. A cool breeze circled around her knees, causing the hairs on the back of her neck to stand on end.

The narrow corridor ran the length of the front of the house, intersecting with another hallway that led to the back of the house. They stood at the crossroads in the hall, scouting both ways. A door at one end slammed suddenly and Georgia dove into Justin's arms.

"Remind me to thank the ghost," he said quietly, resting his chin on the top of her head as he held her close. His quiet laugh reverberated against her heart.

"We could both be devoured by zombies at any moment and all you can think of is me clinging to you like a wet monkey?" She looked up and met his heated gaze.

"Hey, can't blame a guy for having a dying wish."

"Will you go find out what…or who…shut that door?" She gave him a pointed look.

He grabbed her chin and tilted her face to his, capturing her mouth in a quick but thorough kiss. "Just in case." He started down the hall.

Following quietly on his heels, a million scenarios took flight in her mind—from a vagrant passing through to an escaped convict, maybe a wild bear, or worse, a ghost.

She fisted the back of Justin's shirt as he eased the door open, its old hinges squeaking loudly through the silent house.

"Oh, my God," he screamed, throwing open the door.

Georgia screamed, and without thought, pushed ahead and freed herself from the blanket, wadding it in front of her like a stubby, sagging sword.

Justin raced by her, planting one foot on the old mattress on the bed as he swatted at a furry brown animal searching for an escape through the partially open window. The gauzy white curtain, hanging torn on the rod, waved happily in the breeze.

Georgia stared at the sight, observing in what seemed to be slow motion Justin battling the squirrel until it finally leapt out the window. Victory won, she wrapped the blanket around her shoulders and sat on the edge of the bed in an attempt to get her heart under control.

Justin stood at the window laughing his ass off. He walked around the edge of the bed, still laughing. The man had tears forming at the corners of his eyes.

"I'm glad you think it's funny." Georgia glanced at him as he sat down beside her. She debated whether to shove him out the window after the varmint or toss him back on the bed and relieve the tension she'd been repressing.

"Oh, my God, that was priceless," he said, brushing his eyes with the back of his hand.

She punched his shoulder. "You were just hoping that's what I would do."

His laughter dissolved. "Maybe I was." He touched her shoulder and, despite the blanket barrier, her skin erupted in gooseflesh. She shivered.

He dropped his arm behind her and leaned close, pushing his face to hers. "Come on, admit it was funny. The look on your face"—he tucked an errant wisp of hair over her ear— "was…is…beautiful."

"You're an ass," she said, eying him as he drew close. His gaze lingered a moment on her mouth before meeting her eyes.

"I think maybe you kind of like that, Georgie," he said, softly touching his lips to hers.

She reached up to touch his firm jaw. She'd always loved his mouth, the shape, how it fit to hers. He eased her back on the bed, slipping his hand beneath the opening of the blanket, slowly caressing her with each kiss, freeing her inhibitions.

He pulled back and searched her eyes. "I never thought

a pair of boots and underwear would turn me on, but damn, woman, you've got me turned inside out and I'm not sure what to do about it."

She wrapped her hand around his neck, pulling him onto a fiery kiss. "I think you can figure it out, cowboy."

He swallowed hard, holding her gaze, his blue eyes smoldering heat. "Keep your boots on."

"Only if you do." She sighed as he drew down the lacy top of her bra, freeing one rosy tip. Lavishing her with teeth and tongue, he kissed his way to her panties, drawing them down with his teeth.

The wicked grin as he looked up at her was enough to make her wet. Tossing aside what clothes she wore, he assisted her in drawing his T-shirt over his head, and welcomed him into another passionate kiss. The weight of him felt glorious, the hard muscle of his body pressing to hers. He covered the juncture between her thighs, tracing the warmth with his fingers as he kissed his way down her belly, rubbing his unshaven jaw against her sensitive flesh, causing a slow burn to rise as he pleasured her.

Georgia was lost in a euphoric haze. Hooking her boot heels to the bedsprings, she grabbed at the blanket, her body writhing to his loving touch. She'd lost her virginity to him years ago, as a boy, and now she was losing her mind to his skills as a mature lover.

"My sweet Georgie," he whispered, his hot breath searing her flesh.

She glanced down, aware of every sensation, her heart overjoyed that it was Justin summoning these wonderful sensations, causing the heat to build deep inside her.

"That's it, sweetheart," he said, moving over her, crushing his mouth to hers as he plunged two fingers deep, bringing her to dizzying heights. She fell apart in a blur of laughter and tears, blindly reaching for his belt. "Lord in heaven, tell me you have protection."

He stood, shoving his jeans down, and sheathed himself in short order before covering her body with his, pushing in fully to the hilt.

She closed around him, milking him with another climax.

"Jesus. Georgie," he gasped, building to a slow rhythm.

She held him, not wanting to let go. How could she watch him leave again? She shoved the thought away, wanting this moment with him—even if it was to be the last time.

·ᓚᘏᗢ·

JUSTIN'S BODY STOOD AT THE edge of a cliff. This was Georgia. *His* Georgia. He kissed her softly, searching those beautiful eyes as richly colored as any pine forest. He wanted her to remember this, to claim her, to spoil her for anyone else.

They moved in tandem, what he'd once felt for her in the beginning reawakened with each tender kiss, each look, each whispered word. He loved her then, and he realized the truth—he was still in love with her.

"Justin," she said, framing his face, then sighed as another climax claimed her body. His body broke free, and he drove hard, giving in to his own release, his body loving her with everything he had. "I love you, Georgie," he said though the haze of lust in his brain.

Only then did he realize Georgie's quiet sobbing. "Georgie, honey, you okay?"

She pushed gently against his shoulders and sat up. Quickly grabbing her underwear and drawing the blanket around her, she hurried downstairs.

By the time he'd pulled himself together, she was

dressed, the blanket wadded in her arms as though shielding herself. "I need to go now, Justin. I need to get home."

He was confused by her reaction to what he'd felt was an amazing breakthrough in their relationship—that suddenly, he realized, seemed very one-sided. Maybe he'd only seen, only felt, what he wanted to see and feel. Dammit.

Neither spoke on the drive in the aftermath of the storm. There was no magical sunset to end this illusion. No holding hands, no quiet smiles, no heated glances.

He followed her to the front door in more of an attempt to keep pace with her than enjoying the moment they'd shared. Part of him wondered if she was thinking of the funeral, when they'd made love and then things had changed. As far as he was concerned, that wasn't going to happen this time. Not unless, of course, it was her that walked away. A cold dread formed in his gut at the very real possibility.

"It was really nice to see you, Justin." She had her hand on the doorknob.

Nice? "Hey, wait a minute, aren't we going to talk about this?"

She hesitated, then met his gaze. "I wish this could work, but it can't."

He frowned. How could she ignore what had just happened? "What do you mean…can't?" He cupped her shoulders, forcing her to look at him. "Don't you think we ought to at least give this a shot?" In his confusion, his ire rose. Maybe this was all a mistake. Maybe she was somehow still involved with Kolby's dad. "Hey, if this is someone else…."

She shook her head, but looked away. "I need to go."

"Will I see you at the reunion dance tomorrow night?" he asked.

"Yes, but I'll be working." She quickly met his gaze. "Good night, Justin. I had a nice time."

If he heard that word once more he might tear the door off its hinges. Frustrated, he watched dumbfounded as she shut the door behind her.

He arrived back at his brother's house to find it empty. Jake wasn't home yet and he found a note from Faith that she had a neighborhood alliance meeting and that he and Jake were on their own for supper.

He was just as grateful to have the time alone. Grabbing a beer, he stepped onto the covered patio and tried to figure out when things had gone sideways. He flopped down in one of the chairs and let his gaze drift to the smattering of stars beginning to peep through the remaining storm clouds. He'd overreacted one time to a rumor and look at the heartache and wasted time that had gotten him. He was determined not to jump to conclusions this time. Taking a pull on his beer, he gazed at the old dogwood tree in the backyard, its delicate, white petals littering the ground, victims of the wind and rain, leaving behind their heady scent.

"Hey, there you are. Didn't expect to see you back so soon." Jake, drink in hand, sat down on the couch across from him. He pointed at Justin's beer. "See you started without me. How'd your day go?"

Justin cocked his head and chuckled. He took a long drink before he spoke. "You know, I must not remember Mom and Dad's relationship very well. It didn't seem that complicated to me. Did you ever sense that?"

"So, that good of a day, huh?" Jake answered.

Justin shook his head. "The woman confuses me."

"I find most women confusing." Jake raised his glass. "That said, and more to your question, I'm sure Mom and Dad had their moments." Jake offered a short laugh. "Why do you suppose Mom spent so much time helping at that ranch on weekends?"

"Oh, come on," Justin argued. "Mom loved being around horses. You know that."

"True. But that happens, buddy. The honeymoon wears off and suddenly you realize you're two very different people with different likes and dislikes."

"Are you talking about your own marriage? Because in case you hadn't noticed, your wife is pretty damn amazing," Justin pointed his beer bottle at his brother.

"Nice of you to notice." He grinned. "And yes, I know she is. I won't argue that. I am one lucky SOB to have someone like Faith. But we're confident enough in our marriage to allow each other the freedom to explore who we are as individuals."

"You think that's what Mom and Dad did?" Justin hadn't thought much about what had kept his parents together.

Jake struck a thoughtful pose. "I can't say. Dad could be mean. Especially when he'd been drinking. I think after we grew up and we no longer needed twenty-four-seven care by Mom, she needed something else to care for."

"You think she loved Dad?"

Jake nodded. "Yeah. The business changed him from the man she fell in love with, in my opinion. But Mom believed in the sanctity of marriage. She advised me early on that, if it was important enough to you, then it was worth working through the issues."

Justin raised a brow. "You think the business has changed you?"

"Now, funny you should ask that. I realized something today," Jake said.

"Yeah?"

"I realized today that it'd been too long since I'd had a picnic with my wife…not to mention what followed."

Justin cringed. "Too much information." Still, he was glad to hear that Jake had reassessed his goals.

He nodded. "Yep. I've decided to make a couple of changes. First, I'm taking off a day a week. Second, I'm going to start delegating some of these business trips. Third, I've decided it's time we started a family. I mean, Faith and I aren't getting any younger, right?"

"Maybe you, bro," Justin grinned.

Jake flipped him the bird.

Justin nodded and blew out a long sigh. Hell, if Jake and Faith could work things out, if his parents who'd been married forty some-odd years could work out their differences, then maybe there was still hope for things to work out between him and Georgia—assuming that both of them were willing to do so. "I really thought things were going well today." Justin glanced at his brother. "We drove out to the old Stoneville house."

Jake spewed part of his drink, dabbing his chin. "You don't waste any time."

"It started as a picnic…and you're welcome. Faith thought the idea sounded romantic."

"And was it?" Jake smiled.

"None of your business," Justin said.

Jake's grin widened.

"I don't want to lose her again. If that means I have to move back here to prove to her that I'm serious, then by God, I'm prepared to do that."

"Have you told her that?" Jake asked.

"She hasn't given me the chance."

"There is a kid to think of. That could be tough. And you don't have any idea what her life with his father… what I mean is, maybe he's still involved somehow."

"She claims he's not. But she won't talk to me about it."

Jake studied him. "Well, I guess this is one of those times

when you need to ask yourself how important she is to you—and her son, since they're a package deal."

⌘

THE NEXT EVENING AS JUSTIN finished trimming his beard, his cell phone rang. He glanced at the screen, recognizing his mother's number. "Hey, Mom."

"Thought I'd call and see how things are in Atlanta. Tonight's your reunion dinner dance, right?"

Since his mother's move to the eastern side of the state, he'd made it a habit to call her every couple of weeks and had spent holidays there with her and his aunt. Only once in that entire time had she ever mentioned Georgia Langley and he'd decidedly put the kibosh on the subject, stating that he didn't wish to speak about her. Justin knew the phone call out of the blue was mom-code for "have you and your brother patched things up yet?"

"Well, one would assume that since you're still there after two days' time, you and your brother are getting along?" she asked.

He smiled. She'd miscarried once before conceiving twins. As it turned out, they were to be their only children and she treated them like everything else in her life—with precious respect and care. She was, and always would be, the heart of their family.

"We're okay." Justin heard her soft sigh of reassurance.

"Good, I'm glad. Life's too short to let wounds fester."

"And it helps that I spoke to Georgia and discovered another side to the information that I was given by Mac."

"You loved that girl, didn't you? I remember how that news broke your heart."

Justin glanced at the clock. He'd hoped to get to the

reunion early enough to speak privately with Georgia. Nonetheless, he wasn't quite ready to share with his mom that he still loved that girl. "I know, but life goes on and we're all grown up now."

A brief silence followed. "If it's important to you, son, you'll find a way through the issues."

He could never get anything past her.

"Thanks, Mom. Give Aunt Irene a hug for me. Talk to you soon."

He hung up, renewed in the hope that fate might be giving him a chance to make Georgia an offer she couldn't refuse.

He had to give Jolie credit. She'd turned the plain hall into a masterful illusion of twinkling lights, music, and a banquet feast fit for royalty. Miniature lights prevailed inside and out, covering trees, potted plants, even the shrubbery along the walkways. A spectacular canopy of lights came to a focal point on the ceiling above the guest tables, creating a sparkling chandelier overhead. On either side of the room were long tables laden with the best of southern cuisine, and a small dance floor with a DJ was set up at the far end of the room.

In the opposite corner, he spotted the cash bar, brought in by Langley's. Several of her staff, dressed in smart black-and-white attire, moved through the crowd serving champagne to guests.

Justin took a deep breath and started across the room, only to be waylaid by classmates who'd arrived early. Mac and Jolie were among them. Mac caught his attention and waved him over to the table where he and Jolie sat.

"Hey, we saved you a seat here, and ones for Jake and Faith, too. Are they here yet?"

Seeing the two of them together seemed profoundly logical. Justin hadn't anticipated how he'd feel seeing Mac again. He didn't want to get into it tonight with Mac. He just wanted to talk with Georgia. "Uh, yeah. They were right behind me. If you'll excuse me."

Mac hopped up from his seat and cut Justin off. "Hey, I don't know if you've seen her, but Georgia looks very hot tonight. I mean, if I wasn't here with Jolie, I'd think about asking her out. What do you think? Would that be, you know, okay with you?" He grinned.

Justin curled his hand into a tight fist at his side. The look on his face must have revealed his true thoughts.

Mac frowned. "Hey, there's nothing going on between you two, is there? I mean, like that was over years ago—even before the whole thing with your brother. You know, before he got married."

Justin summoned every ounce of patience he had and took a step closer to Mac. He leaned forward, cheek to cheek with him, so no one would hear him. "Mac, you're damn lucky I don't take you outside right now and beat the shit out of you. That crap you told me about Georgia and Jake wasn't even remotely accurate and I've spent way too many years estranged from my brother because of it. Now, that part is on me and I'm taking steps to resolve it. But, more importantly, there's a woman here who deserves an apology from you. Because those rumors hurt Georgia deeply and she didn't deserve it. So, here's my advice and I'll say it once—get a life and stay away from Georgia." He straightened and looked into Mac's shocked face. "Do we have an understanding?" Justin asked quietly.

"Hey, man, I didn't know. When Jake told me what had happened, I just assumed—"

"You assumed wrong." Justin held his gaze.

Mac swallowed. "Jesus, I'm sorry."

"Don't apologize to me, Mac." He stepped around his flustered classmate, leaving him to deal with how to resolve his guilt. He looked up and found Georgia across the room, her head down, looking at a clipboard. She wore a short black dress with black-heeled sandals that made her legs seem a mile long. She'd covered her dress with a full, white apron. "Hey." He walked up to her. "I was hoping we might have a few minutes to talk?"

"I'm sorry, Justin. It's not a good time." She gave him a cursory glance.

"Maybe later, then? You could save me a dance?" he offered with a smile.

She didn't look up. "I'm sorry, really." She peered around him, seemingly to speak with another. "Jolie, are the servers getting the champagne out to guests per your instructions?"

Justin stepped aside so the two women could talk. Jolie smiled up at him. She was carrying two flutes of bubbly. "Almost," she said, holding the glass out to him. "Can I steal you away just a bit, honey?" Jolie asked, hooking her arm through his. "I want to run a wonderful idea past you." She glanced at Georgia. "You don't mind, do you, Georgia?"

Georgia glanced at her clipboard and shrugged.

To hell with this. Justin untangled himself from Jolie's grip, grabbed Georgia's clipboard, and slapped it on the bar.

Tank, who'd been standing a few feet away, looked up.

"Can you handle things while I speak with your boss for a moment?" He met Georgia's gaze. "I only need five minutes."

"B-but," Jolie sputtered as Justin shoved the glass back in her hand.

Mac appeared at Justin's side, pushing through to Georgia. He took her hands in his. "I swear on my father's grave, I had no idea how much my big mouth had hurt you. I was wrong to assume what had happened between you and Jake. God, if there is any way I can make it up to you, just say the word. As God is my witness, I thought things were over then between you and Justin."

Was the world going mad? Justin met Tank's gaze.

The big man walked over and turned Georgia in Justin's direction. Placing his hand on Mac's chest, he gave Georgia a nudge and Justin caught her hand. "Now, what can I fix for you two?" He grinned at Jolie and Mac.

Seizing the opportunity, Justin dragged her through the open side doors and into the private garden area outside. He faced her then. "Look, Georgia, I don't know what's going on between us. But I feel something and I don't want it to slip away. Not again. Not if there's even the remote chance you may feel the same."

"Justin," she said wearily, folding her arms over her chest. "There have only been two men—besides Kolby—that I've loved in my life. You were my first love and always will be."

His hopes lifted as he reached for her.

"After everything that happened between us, I never thought that I could love anyone as much…not until I met Caleb."

His hands dropped to their sides.

One of the Langley servers appeared at the double-wide entrance. "My apologies, Ms. Langley, but we've got a bit of a crisis going on inside. We need you."

Caleb? Justin was still reeling from the bomb she'd dropped.

"I'm sorry, I need to go." She turned on her heel to leave. He grabbed her hand.

"After the party. We need to talk."

"I'll…think about it." She walked away, leaving him shell-shocked.

He barely touched any food, had no appetite for it. Instead, he took a long walk alone in the neighborhood, giving him time to think. He returned to the reunion late and found Faith seated alone at a table. "Mind if I join you?" he asked.

"Please do. I figured you were over there reliving the glory days with the rest of the team."

Justin smiled and glanced over at the throng of males, laughing and drinking, growing louder with each toast to the good old days. He shook his head. "I only played football because Jake asked me to. I really preferred track."

She leaned over and patted his hand, and he thought he saw the glimmer of tears in her eyes.

"Hey, are you okay?" he asked, dropping his hand over hers. "You need me to get Jake?"

"No." She tugged on his hand as he started to rise. He returned to his seat.

She searched his eyes as though debating whether to confide in him. "I found out today I'm pregnant." Her smile was wobbly, at best. She blinked and glanced away, dabbing her eyes with a napkin. She let out a short laugh. "The thing is, I'm not sure Jake's going to be happy about it."

"Oh, sweetheart." Justin slid into the chair next to her and put his arm around her shoulders. "He's going to be nuts. He was just telling me last night that he wanted to start a family."

"He did?" She sniffed.

Justin nodded. "That, amongst some other changes that I think are great. You guys are going to be great parents." He patted her shoulder.

"Making moves again on my wife, I see." Jake clamped one hand on Justin's shoulder. "You don't mind if I ask her to dance, do you?" Jake kissed the top of his brother's head. "I love you, bro." Then he held his hand out to Faith.

Justin was unable to keep from smiling as he saw Jake pull Faith close and watched the transformation on his face as she told him her news.

At that moment, he realized how badly he wanted that with Georgia. But it was too late. Never mind what had happened between them yesterday. Some guy named Caleb had already claimed her heart.

Chapter Five

GEORGIA HAD SEEN THE HURT on Justin's face when she mentioned Caleb's name. Maybe it was better to make him believe that her heart still belonged to another. Part of her would always love Caleb—for forcing her to move on, to love again, and, of course, for Kolby. But she and Kolby had managed just fine on their own, without a man in their lives.

"How are you holding up, sweetheart?"

Tank stood at her side. The night had been profitable for this new portable bar catering venture. Aside from the income from the cash bar and the set-up fee charged to the reunion committee, she and Tank had exchanged a good number of business cards and phone numbers regarding potential new clients.

She leaned on the bar and slipped off her shoes. "These heels are killing me."

"Never understood why women tortured themselves with those stiletto heels." Tank glanced at her. "Unless, of course, the woman is trying to make an impression." He raised one silvery brow over his steely, blue-eyed gaze.

"Please," she answered, rotating her ankle to ease the stiff soreness. Nothing that a good soak in the tub and a glass of wine couldn't cure. Her heart…now, that was a different matter.

"Saw you talking to that guy...what's his name? Jasper?"

"Justin." Georgia tossed him a side look. Tank knew his name by now—probably his shirt size and birthday too, given his military resources.

"So, things going okay there?" he asked casually, handing a guest a wine spritzer.

"What are you, my dad?" She watched her classmates dancing the night away, watched them laughing with one another, connecting. She felt none of that.

"Well, I'd like to think I'm more of a big brother, thank you, very much," Tank said, then sighed. "Look, if he's bothering you, he and I could have a little chat, you know?" Tank's somber expression reflected his seriousness.

Georgia faced him. "You know, you scare me sometimes with how protective you are." She smiled. "Listen, you are a dear, dear friend. You were to my dad, and always have been the same to me. And I want you to know how much I appreciate your offer, but I think I can handle this."

The big man smiled and tapped his knuckles on the counter of the bar. "I'm here if you need me." His gaze lifted to the room filled with guests. "Looks like you're going to get that chance to handle things soon." He walked away as Justin made his way through the crowd toward her.

"I know you're working, but it's the last song and I wondered if you'd care to dance?" He held out his hand.

Caught without her shoes or excuse to turn him down, she removed her apron and bent down to retrieve her sandals.

"Don't bother," he said, toeing off his shiny oxfords. "These things are killing me." He took her hand. "Come on." He led her to a cluster of lighted potted palms. "You know, I haven't had the chance to tell you how beautiful you look tonight."

He drew her close and she remembered the heat of his body against hers. The music began and her heart stopped at the familiar song. She lowered her head, reprimanding herself for the tears the song prompted. It had been one that Caleb sang, knowing how much she loved the Garth Brooks tune "The Dance".

"Georgie?" Justin searched her face. "Honey, what is it?"

She sniffed and tried to hold in her emotions. "That song…it's…it's hard for me. Caleb—" She had no sooner spoken his name when Justin stepped away.

"I understand."

"No, you don't. But it's time you did." She pulled him outside into the garden. One couple, talking quietly, meandered back inside as she led him to a concrete bench. "Please sit down. I need to share this."

He in his stocking feet, her barefoot, they sat side-by-side on the bench. "You remember me telling you how I was feeling vulnerable that night with your brother?"

He nodded.

"Well, it's because I'd just found out I was pregnant." She cleared her throat. "Let me start over."

Justin looked at her. "Georgia, you don't owe me any explanations."

She took his hand. "I know, but I want you to understand. I need you to understand, okay?"

"Okay."

"I'd been taking on more and more responsibility that year at the bar. Dad was getting forgetful. His health hadn't been good. He'd been actively looking for acts to bring in for the weekends. Caleb was on tour, trying to get a start. Playing every honkytonk from here to Texas, trying to build a following." She smiled at the memory of their first meeting. "He had dreams of making it big in Nashville."

Georgia looked over to see Justin bent forward, his

hands clasped over his knees as she'd seen him do countless times before. She loved how he focused on listening when she really needed him.

"We fell in love. Hard and fast," she continued. "He asked me to go with him, finish out his tour, then come to Nashville." She sighed. "Of course, I couldn't leave, not with Dad's health in decline. He needed me."

Justin nodded.

"He made a promise to come back after the tour was done. By that time, he said I could get some help for Dad and go with him to Nashville." She paused, having never told another soul aside from Aunt Mae and Tank what had happened next. Georgia drew in a breath, summoning her strength. "Two days later, I got a call from Caleb's manager. He told me that the old bus they'd been driving had been broadsided by a semi-truck coming onto the highway from a mountain on-ramp. He'd apparently fallen asleep at the wheel and pressed the accelerator. He hit the side of the bus and pushed them both through the guardrail and over the side of the mountain ravine. There were no survivors."

She looked up and met Justin's horrified expression. "Georgie," he said softly. "I'm so sorry." He hesitated at first, then slid closer and took her in his arms.

She pulled from his embrace and continued. "About a month later, around the time your brother was to get married, I discovered I was pregnant." She chuckled quietly. "I suppose the fact that I started showing a few months later didn't help the rumors any."

Justin shook his head. "I had no idea about any of this."

She shrugged. "Why would you? By then, you'd already moved to Montana and were quite happy to be there, as I understood."

"Even after how I treated you after the funeral, you

were curious about my happiness?" he asked with a half-smile.

"Your old coach came into the bar now and again." She gave him a soft smile and continued. "But there's something else." She looked at him. "When Kolby was three, I started noticing little bruises on him. But, you know, with him being an active little kid, I didn't pay much attention to it. And then one day he had a seizure and, while in the hospital, they diagnosed him with ALL—acute lymphoblastic leukemia." She wrung her hands clasped in her lap. "Apparently, it's one of the common childhood cancers… who knew, right?"

He took her hand, brushing his thumb gently over her knuckles. Calmed by the small bit of connection, she gathered the strength to continue. "It has something to do with the blood cells, primarily. He's already been through so much just to get him to a point of remission. Now the goal is to keep him there, so he can rebuild healthy cells."

"Jesus, he's only five." Justin squeezed her hand.

She nodded, holding back the emotions this conversation had stirred inside her—feelings of guilt, anger, and a profound sadness. If she were to lose Kolby now—Georgia shut her eyes, pushing the thought away. "They tell me that he has a good chance at survival. A few years ago, they gave kids like him a ten percent chance. Now, it's about ninety percent or better."

"Is there anything I can do, Georgie?" Justin said. "Any way I can help?" His blue eyes studied hers. "My God, you're a remarkable woman to have managed all this and a business on your own."

"I've had help. Tank is my rock at work. Aunt Mae"—she shook her head—"I don't know what I'd do without her."

He held her face and kissed her softly. "I love you. I said

it earlier, and I meant it, Georgia Langley. I don't think I've ever stopped loving you. I want to make this work. I want to be there for you and Kolby." He held her gaze. "Listen, my ranch back in End of the Line is a beautiful little place. I've got plenty of room, lots of space for a little kid to play. Lots of fresh air. There's even an equestrian ranch where I work that I bet Kolby would love. And I've got a few horses, I could teach Kolby to ride." He smiled.

Georgia swallowed the lump in her throat and touched his cheek. "You are the sweetest man. But I can't just leave the business and Aunt Mae." Tears slipped down her cheeks. "But I love you for asking."

He grabbed her hands. "Okay, at least promise me that you'll come up for a visit. Bring Kolby. See what you think. Honey, it's what that song is all about—not taking one minute for granted, or the things you have right in front of you. Because none of us knows how much time we've been given."

She leaned her forehead to his. "You're a good man, Justin. You always have been."

"I want to be more to you, Georgie," he said quietly. "If you'll let me."

She offered him a tender kiss as the houselights in the ballroom came up. "Stay with me tonight. I don't want to be alone."

꿁

HE WOKE IN THE DOUBLE bed of the apartment at Langley's alone, his body still charged from making love into the wee hours of the morning with Georgia. He caught the scent of coffee brewing, bacon in a frying pan, and slipped on his boxer briefs before following his nose to the tiny apartment kitchen. He discovered her at the stove, scrambling eggs.

Wrapping his arms around her, he nuzzled her neck. "You smell like bacon." He kissed the ticklish spot beneath her ear. "And you're wearing my T-shirt."

She glanced up at him, set the pan aside, and turned off the stove. "I guess you're just going to have to wrestle me for it." She grinned and side-stepped around him, taking off down the short hall.

"You know I made state in wrestling my junior year," he called out as he started after her. His shirt, flying through the air, slapped him in the face. God almighty, he loved this woman.

Two hours later, they sat on the couch eating fresh scrambled eggs and warmed up coffee. Justin took another stab at suggesting she come up to the ranch, certain that once she experienced the air, the space, the friendly town—and hopefully his presence—she'd consider making it permanent. He had his work cut out for him; he was no fool. She wouldn't ever leave the bar—it was her dad's legacy, and she'd just gotten a good start on her new catering enterprise.

"Look, Georgie. It's summer. Things are a little slow around here. Maybe you and Kolby could come up for a week. I could take him fly fishing."

She leaned over and touched his hand. "You're sweet, Justin. But I don't see how—"

"Yeah, the business." He eyed her. "Fine. Then I guess you leave me no choice. I'll go back to End of the Line, make a few arrangements, and move back here as soon as possible. I can teach anywhere." He shrugged. "Doesn't have to be Montana."

"No, I won't allow it. You love it there."

"I love you more," he said.

"Please, this is happening so fast. I need some time to

think things through," she said.

"Okay." He nodded, but he wasn't giving up. "I'll give you a month." He reached for her and drew her onto his lap. "A month, without this." He framed her face and moved his mouth over hers, catching her heated gaze. "And this—" He slipped his hands beneath her shirt, raking his thumbs across her unencumbered breasts.

"This isn't fair," she said with a sigh.

"Oh, sweetheart, I don't plan to make this easy for you." He turned her beneath him on the couch.

"You're crazy, you know that?" She smiled, sliding down the zipper of his jeans.

"Yes, I am. About you, darlin'." And he proceeded to remind her what she'd miss—what they'd both miss—when he left.

◈

"IT'S GOOD TO SEE YOUR face around here again," Betty said, handing him a fresh cup of coffee. He hadn't asked for it, but Betty must have felt he needed it. Truth was, he hadn't slept in days with Georgia on his mind.

"Thanks, Betty, it's good to be back. Forgot how clean the air is up here." Justin grinned. God knows he'd spent enough time sitting on his front porch swing at night, debating calling Georgia, trying to give her time to think things through.

The bell above the diner clattered and in walked Rein Mackenzie, his brother Dalton, and another man who he'd seen from time to time around town, mostly in the company of the Kinnison brothers.

"Hey, Coach." Rein spotted him and walked to the booth. "You still want me to take a look at building some new benches in the locker room up there at school?"

Justin nodded. "Definitely. Maybe sometime next week we could head up there and I could let you take a look at the old benches. See what I have in mind, or if it'll work. Then I'll present the bid to the school board."

Dalton and the other man joined them. Rein looked over his shoulder. "Coach, you remember my brother Dalton, and this is Hank Richardson."

Hank held out his hand in greeting. "I'm a pseudo-transplant from Chicago," he said, grinning. "I run a private plane charter business."

"Transplant from Atlanta, Georgia," Justin offered, shaking the man's hand. "Private plane? That's impressive. Also, good to know." He wondered how long of a flight it was to Atlanta.

"We went to school with Hank. Lately, he's been here so much, we think he ought to just make the move." Dalton grinned and clamped his hand down on Hank's shoulder.

"Yeah, well, there's a lot to consider when making a major move." Hank shot Dalton a friendly grin. "Good to meet you, Coach."

Justin sensed there was more to that story, but given due time he was likely to hear about it—probably from Betty.

"We'll talk later," Rein said, touching the end of his Stetson.

The door opened again, sending the bell clanging happily after another patron. Looking up, he saw his friend Leslie hurrying over to the booth. She dropped her massive purse on the chair and slid in across from him.

"Sorry I'm late." She held her hands up in defense. "Consulting a young woman who's been through the mill. Just moved here." She glanced thoughtfully at the three men who'd just taken their seats a few tables away, and then shrugged. "You can't rush that kind of conversation." Breathing out a short sigh, she folded her hands and looked at him. "And how about you? Heard anything from Georgia?"

He'd told her everything—well, almost everything—that had happened over the Atlanta weekend. "It's been more than a week. I gave her a month to decide." He cringed and shook his head. "Maybe that wasn't the smartest thing to do."

His friend laid her hand on his. "I could tell you to have faith. I could tell you that what will be, will be. And both are true, to a certain extent. But right now, it doesn't keep you from wondering if you did the right thing, laying your soul bare to someone."

He met her concerned gaze. "You're right about that. I bet I've asked myself a hundred times—what the heck were you thinking?"

His friend smiled. "But if you never take the risk, you'll never reap the reward."

"I guess that's supposed to make me feel better?" He smiled ruefully. It didn't really, but her concern and friendship did. Just having someone to bounce his troubles off of was a great relief.

"Well, that's what they told us in psych class," she answered with a grin.

"Good evening, Reverend," Betty said, bringing a fresh pot of coffee and two clean mugs to the table. She eyed Justin's untouched coffee. "Figured you needed a fresh cup, given the way you been staring at that one since you sat down." She smiled as she placed two steaming cups in front of them. "Now, may I recommend tonight's special—Jerry's chicken n' dumplings with cornbread and your choice of cooked greens or a house salad." She looked from one to the other. "You all look like you're trying to solve world peace over here."

Leslie smiled. "Make that two specials, Betty. With pie. Solving world peace is hard work."

Betty glanced at Justin. "Sounds like matters of the heart." She nodded. "Comfort and joy, coming right up."

Justin looked at Leslie. "You realize I'm going to have to add an extra mile to my morning run?"

She waved away his comment. "That's what friends are for."

Chapter Six

IT'D BEEN WELL OVER A week or better since Justin returned to Montana. She'd staved off Kolby's pleas to go for a visit so he could ride horses and he'd been exemplary in keeping his toys picked up and eating his vegetables to try to influence her decision.

Aunt Mae had said little, but once or twice had let slip that fresh air and visiting a real ranch might be good for his health.

Georgia missed Justin. She missed their late-night talks after they made love, how he made her laugh, how he'd listen patiently when she needed someone to hear her concerns. He lived honestly, loved with all his heart, and he wanted to take care of her and Kolby—he wanted to become a family.

The thought crossed her mind, too, that she was young enough to have another child. But with what losses she'd been through—her father and Caleb—and battling her son's deadly disease, her heart was weary, afraid. It seemed as though everything she'd ever loved had been taken from her, too soon.

Friday afternoon, she decided to go to the bar before opening. Rolling up her sleeves, she embraced the solitude and dove into a deep cleansing which often helped her think things through. Today, however, the silence seemed deafening. She felt alone and lonely.

Determined to get past it, she flipped on the old radio and hummed along as she set to the task of polishing down the old mahogany bar and its brass work. She remembered her father's excitement when he'd found it at an auction. She smiled at the memory. Lord, how he loved coming here every night. The friends he'd made, the fights he'd averted, the aspiring acts to whom he'd given a venue in which to play their music.

"And now it's time to give away tickets for that big tour y'all have been waiting for." The radio DJ's voice crackled over the airwaves. "We've got two tickets to see the great G.B. in person to the first caller who can name this tune."

The familiar piano melody started and Georgia's hand stopped. Was it fate that this song should play at this moment?

Her gaze lifted, her life clarifying in the next instant. She scanned the empty tables, the old dart board where countless patrons had challenged each other, the small stage where she'd first watched Caleb and his band—along with dozens of others—in search for their dream. Langley's…this business…had been her dad's dream.

What was her dream? For herself? For her son?

"You know, I've considered many times talking to you about this idea I had. Never got around to it, until now. So, I figure, I'll give it a shot. What can you do, fire me?"

Startled from her reverie, Georgia turned to find Tank standing at the other end of the bar.

"I wondered if you'd ever thought about going into partnership with me? I could chip in half and take on more of the management." He walked over, leaned his elbow on the bar, and looked at her. "It'd give you a little nest egg—to, I don't know, do some traveling. Maybe spend a little more time with your son?"

Tears welled in her eyes. With crystal clarity, she saw the chance she'd been given—perhaps her last—not only to find love again with her first love, but to become a family, giving her the opportunity to provide Kolby a quality of life that she'd not be able to if working here twenty-four-seven.

She offered Tank a wobbly smile, walked over and hugged his waist, as far as her arms would reach around the big man. "So, you think that now's a good time to spring this on me, why?"

Tank cleared his throat and held her at arm's length. "It might have had something to do with the numerous phone calls I've had with that cowboy of yours."

Georgia's heart did a little flip. "Justin?"

Tank shrugged. "Yeah, well, I'd been kicking the idea around for a while now, waiting for the right time. You haven't been ready to let go a little. Delegate."

"But what about the bills?" She shook her head. "We're already behind." She returned to robustly polishing the bar. "I can't just up and leave you like that."

Tank lifted his bushy eyebrows. "Yeah, that's why it'd be smart to bring in an investor."

She shot him a curious look. "Wait, what do you mean an investor?"

He lifted his bushy brows and cocked his head. "Someone who'd foot the bill for marketing, do a little advertising for us. Help to get the catering business off the ground."

Georgia laughed outright. Neither of them knew anyone with that kind of clout.

Voices filtered from down the back hall as Jake Reed, his wife, Faith, and Mac appeared, walking up to the bar. Jake looked at Tank. "You tell her yet?"

"Just getting to that part," Tank tossed him a side look.

"Oh." He made a face like he'd let the cat out of the

bag.

"Is someone going to tell me what is going on?" She planted her fist, the cloth, and her pride on her hip. This whole matter smacked too close of something being taken away without her consent. She didn't like that.

Faith slid onto the bar stool as Mac and Jake stood behind her. "Georgia," she began, "we want to help. We know how you feel about this place. How important it is for you to preserve what you and your dad worked so hard to create."

"You ask anyone five miles of this place. It's an icon to the folks who live around here and have been patrons for years," Mac interjected enthusiastically.

"Wanting to help with that isn't so hard to understand, is it?" Faith said with a soft smile. Jake put his hands on her shoulders and kissed his wife's cheek.

Stunned, Georgia scanned their faces. "No, that part isn't hard at all. What I don't understand is why? I'm sorry to be so frank, but why would you care about me or my dad's business?"

Jake looked at her. "I can see where you'd think that, Georgia. But we'd like to put the past where it belongs and start fresh."

She narrowed her gaze. "Why?"

Jake's blue-eyed gaze—so like his brother's—held hers. "Because with any luck, and provided my crazy ass brother isn't delusional, we're going to be family. The man is sitting up there in Big Sky country thinking of you, losing sleep, beside himself with what he should do—and now the calls have started, morning, noon—"

"And night," Faith added with a grin.

"He can't stop thinking about you and Kolby," Jake said. "And I...we"—he gestured to the four of them— "think that maybe you feel something for him, as well. For the love of God, I hope that's the case."

Faith smacked his shoulder.

She couldn't believe her ears. "I don't know what to say."

"Well," Faith, said with a smile, "maybe you should first ask yourself whether or not you love Justin, because I'm pretty sure he's head over heels in love with you."

Georgia swallowed the lump in her throat. "I do."

"Yes-s-s." Jake pumped his fist into the air.

"Oh, thank, God." Mac blew out a sigh.

"He's called you excessively, as well?" Georgia looked at Tank.

The big man rolled his eyes. "Have mercy on me, Georgia," he pleaded with a smile.

She looked from one to the other. "What now?"

Jake took her hand. "You go home. Pack a few things for you and Kolby and catch the next plane to Billings." He squeezed her hand. "He's trying to be patient. Giving you time to think things through. Meanwhile, the rest of us are going through hell here."

Georgia laughed and searched Jake's face. "You're serious?" It would mean being able to spend time with Justin and give Kolby the life she wanted for him, and know still that her business was in good hands.

Jake placed a hand on his chest. "As a heart attack, sweetheart."

"Tank and I will draw up the paperwork and fax it to you, so you can read everything before you decide or want changes. Mac and I have been thinking of pulling in some big names to generate interest as a smaller venue for country singers who, now and again, prefer an intimate setting to sold-out arenas."

Georgia skirted around the end of the bar and hugged each of them. "I don't know how to thank you all…so much."

"By letting us get some sleep, for starters." Jake smiled.

Her heart already felt it had wings. "Okay." She nodded and stuffed the polishing cloth in Mac's hand. "Use only Amish milk on that baby." She looked around her. "I guess I have a plane to catch, but make me a promise. Don't tell Justin I'm coming. I have to do this my way in order to be sure. Are you all with me on this?"

"However you need to do this, we understand." Faith hugged her again. "I've always wanted a sister-in-law," she whispered before letting her go.

Forty-eight hours later, she and Kolby were en route in a rented pick-up from Billings airport to End of the Line, Montana.

"Does this mean I get cowboy boots?" her son asked. He'd been wide awake the entire trip, soaking in every minute. The grin never left his face.

"We'll see." Georgia glanced at him. He'd insisted on wearing the snap-front shirt that Aunt Mae had bought for him. Her aunt had hugged her as they climbed in the cab headed to the airport, promising to ship a few more boxes to her at her word.

"I have a good feeling about that young man," she'd told her.

So did Georgia. She only hoped that, when faced with the reality of seeing them in the flesh, he wouldn't suddenly change his mind. She wanted her dream of a happily ever after.

She stopped at the corner gas station at the edge of End of the Line to let Kolby use the restroom and hopefully get directions to Justin's ranch.

A friendly smile appeared on the dark-haired clerk's face. "You must be Georgia."

Georgia glanced down at Kolby's surprised expression.

"It's your accent. Dead giveaway that you're that southern girl he's been talking about since he got back from Atlanta," the clerk explained. "You know, we used to tease Justin something terrible about his accent when he first moved up here. But you have no worries. We have a lot of transplants here. Folks who visit once, and decide to stay." She held up her hands. "Not in a scary movie kind of way, though. It's just a good little town to raise kids." She peered over the counter. "And you must be?"

"Kolby, ma'am." His tiny voice produced a sweet drawl.

"Aren't you the most adorable thing ever," the woman said as she rifled in a candy dish behind the counter. "I'm Denise," she said as she started to hand a sucker to her son. "Is it okay with you, mama?"

Georgia smiled and nodded. Justin hadn't been kidding when he said the town was friendly.

"So, Justin's place..." She pointed. "Just go out here, take a left. Go up to the square. Take another left and go about a half mile. You can't miss it. Cute little acreage with a lovely white three-story farmhouse, porch swing faces the west."

"Thank you, Denise." Georgia held out her hand. "Nice to meet you."

"You need something we don't have, we can order it by tomorrow."

"Thanks," she said as she ushered Kolby out the door.

A few moments later, she was pulling off the main road onto a gravel lane lined on both sides by white fence, leading up to a large yard and one of the most picturesque views she'd ever seen in her life. The three-story farmhouse had a wraparound porch, complete with a swing as Denise had suggested. Situated a few yards from the house was a barn with a horse paddock beside it. An old, blue Chevy pick-up sat near the house and beyond the fences she noted several horses grazing in the pasture. Behind the scene, rising majestically in the distance, were snow-capped mountains standing sentinel over the valley.

"Is this where Justin lives?" Kolby asked in awe.

"Mr. Reed," Georgia corrected her son. At least for now, she wanted the formality. A movement on the horizon caught her eye and she watched a figure on horseback riding across the plains toward the barn. As the rider drew closer, she saw the cowboy hat and buckskin coat and her heart flipped, falling in love all over again.

He lifted his hand in a wave and Georgia climbed from the truck.

Kolby unbuckled and shimmied down after her.

Justin's grin warmed her as he approached, looking better than any fantasy she could dream up. He brought the horse to a slow walk.

"I see you decided to come. Been thinking an awful lot about you. I've missed you."

Her insides fluttered. She smiled as she shaded her eyes. "So the woman at the Git n' Go told me."

He flashed her a wicked grin, climbed off the horse, and held her gaze as he took off his hat and lifted her off the ground with one arm. He kissed her softly. "I really missed you," he whispered before setting her to her feet.

He knelt down on one knee to address Kolby. "Good to see you again, Kolby. It's nice to know that you were watching over your mom on this trip."

His little chest puffed with pride as he smiled up at him. "Are you a real cowboy?" he asked, his eyes wide behind his thick glasses.

Justin straightened and glanced at her. "Well, I can do a lot of cowboy things. I can even teach you to ride if your mom says it's okay."

Kolby's gaze darted to hers. "Can I?"

"We just got here, honey," she said, smoothing her hand over his short hair still growing in at all directions in the aftermath of the chemotherapy.

"Tell you what," Justin said, climbing back into the saddle. "If Mom doesn't mind, you can sit up here with me and help take Cocoa back to the barn. The we can get you two settled up at the house. You like pizza?"

Both males looked at Georgia for her approval.

She walked over, picked up her son, and lifted him into Justin's strong, grasp. "You ever handle a wiggly five-year-old, Mr. Reed?" She grinned up at him.

He tucked Kolby between him and the saddle horn, and placed a protective hand around the boy's middle. "Now you hold the reins, like this." He smiled down at her. "Is that anything like a busload of high-school boys on their way to a football game?"

"Fair enough," she said, and her heart did a somersault when Kolby turned his little face to Justin's, his expression one of admiration and vibrant joy.

Tears pricked at the back of her eyes as she watched the two guiding the horse back to the barn. She couldn't hear the details of the conversation, only the sound of her son's delighted laughter as Justin brought the horse to a slow trot.

She stood in the dusky shadows and breathed deeply. The summer air was cool, mixed with grass and pine. For the first time in many years, she felt the wall she'd built around her heart crumble and dared to believe she could trust in love again.

The two emerged from the barn a few moments later, walking side-by-side as they talked. No doubt Kolby was riddling him with a thousand questions as he was often prone to do. Suddenly, Justin plopped his hat on Kolby's head and the boy's face lit up in a billion-dollar grin.

She handed Kolby his little backpack. "You can carry this, mister."

Justin leaned down and whispered something to the boy as he pointed toward the house. Kolby grinned and took off at a dead run up the porch steps.

Justin looped his arm around her shoulder and kissed her temple. "I happen to know there are fresh chocolate chip cookies in the kitchen." He turned her into his arms. "So, what do you think? You like it well enough to stay a spell?"

She traced her finger over those lips she'd dreamt of for days—but felt like an eternity. "I might be persuaded."

He lifted a brow and grinned. "Let's get your things inside, then."

She dropped the tailgate to reveal several suitcases and one or two boxes. "You know, my son's going to want cowboy boots and a hat next."

He peered at the number of bags and looked up at her. "A man ought to marry the mother of the boy he plans to teach to ride, don't you think?" He straightened, took her hand, and kissed it. "You let me know if this is going too fast. The way I see it, I don't want to waste another minute without you and Kolby in my life."

She leapt into his arms and hugged his neck. From the porch came the delighted squeal of her son. "I told you she'd say yes!" Kolby said, cupping his hands to his mouth.

"Was there anyone not involved in this?" She grinned and kissed him hard.

"Are we good?" A woman's voice captured Georgia's attention.

She shimmied from his embrace to look at the slender woman with short silvery-colored hair standing next to Kolby, who was bouncing up and down in jubilation.

"Are we good?" Justin asked her.

Georgia nodded. Tears stained her cheeks that hurt from smiling so much.

Justin put his thumb in the air.

"Oh, good! Come on, Kolby." The woman took her son's hand. "Let's go call your Uncle Jake."

"Your mom?" she asked through laughter and tears.

"I swear, she happened to show up on my doorstep this morning. Had no idea. But it's handy to have her here."

"Why's that?"

He pulled out his cell phone. "Aside from the cookies"—he tapped it a few times before setting it on the tailgate— "may I have this dance?" He held out his hand.

It wasn't Garth Brooks. It was Randy Travis, crooning a wedding favorite— "Forever and Ever, Amen".

"Figured we needed a song of our own." He pulled her into his arms. "The rest of the family, Tank, and your Aunt Mae will be here Sunday for the wedding."

"Wedding? You had all this planned?" she asked as they danced against the last dredges of a mountain sunset.

He grinned, then kissed her. "Yes, everything except the part that's up to you. What do you say, Georgia Anne? Do you love me?"

She pulled him close, her heart beating hard against his. "Forever and ever…Amen."

The End

DEAR READERS,
I hope you enjoyed Justin and Georgia's story. And I'm thrilled to announce Georgia and Kolby decided to settle in End of the Line!

Back in December 2016, I introduced readers to End of the Line, Montana through LOST AND FOUND. In April 2017, I followed with another crossover novella, GEORGIA ON MY MIND. Both are part of a new line of books related to both the Kinnison Legacy trilogy, the books that started it all.

As much as I loved writing these characters, it appeared readers did as well, readers asked for more, and so came the spin-off series –Last Hope Ranch was born. This series features guests and those who work directly with the dream Jed Kinnison had for the ranch, to make it a place of healing and second chances for both horse and humans. In NO STRINGS ATTACHED (Sally and Clay's story) I introduced to you, Hank Richardson, and old friend of the Kinnison brothers, and Clay's sister, Julie Williams, who along with her sons, Chris and Kyle, are rescued from a domestic violence stand-off. Now living at Last Hope Ranch, Julie and Hank assess the sparks between them to determine if it's real or simply hero worship. Watch for their story in WORTH THE WAIT, coming in 2017! And in August of 2017, I'll be releasing my second Sable Hunter's Hell Yeah! Kindle World story-HURRICANE SEASON which features Dr. Gavin Beauregard, the new physician at Billings Clinic Hospital (introduced in No Strings Attached) and Caroline Richardson (Hank's little sis and introduced in Rustler's Heart) What does fate, a tropical storm, and tea leaves have in store for these two? Find out in HURRICANE SEASON coming in August to Kindle World.

The KINNSON LEGACY TRILOGY, THE LAST HOPE RANCH, AND THE END OF THE LINE, MONTANA series all feature the familiar faces and introduce new folks who may visit, live, work, love and play in this once booming old mining town!! Come on by! We think you'll like it here!

Amanda

About the Author

AMANDA MCINTYRE'S STORYTELLING IS A natural offshoot of her artistic creativity. A visual writer, living in the rich tapestry of the American heartland, her passion is telling character-driven stories with a penchant (okay, some call it a wicked obsession) for placing ordinary people in extraordinary situations to see how they overcome the obstacles to their HEA. A bestselling author, her work is published internationally in Print, eBook, and Audio. She writes steamy contemporary and sizzling historical romance and truly believes, no matter what, love will always find a way.

Find out how to sign up for my newsletter, follow me on social links, and be included in upcoming announcements at: amandamcintyresbooks.com

Other Books by Amanda McIntyre

CONTEMPORARY WESTERN ROMANCE:

KINNISON LEGACY:
Rugged Hearts, Book I Wyatt & Aimee
Rustler's Heart, Book II Rein & Liberty
Renegade Hearts, Book III Dalton & Angelique
All I Want for Christmas (Kinnison holiday novella)

LAST HOPE RANCH:
No Strings Attached, Book I
Worth the Wait, Book II (2017)

END OF THE LINE, MONTANA:
Lost and Found/Crossover novella
Georgia on My Mind/EOL Crossover Novella (April.2017)
Hurricane Season/EOL crossover/Hell Yeah Kindle World (Aug.2017)

KINDLEWORLD SINGLE TITLE:
Going Home /Sapphire Falls Kindle World
Thunderstruck/Hell Yeah Kindle World

CONTEMPORARY ROMANCE:
Stranger in Paradise

Tides of Autumn
Unfinished Dreams
Wish You Were Here

HISTORICAL:
A Warrior's Heart
The Promise
Closer to You (formerly Wild & Unruly)
Christmas Angel (formerly Fallen Angel)
Tirnan 'Oge
The Dark Seduction of Miss Jane

HARLEQUIN SPICE/HISTORICAL:
The Master & the Muses ★(audio/international)
The Diary of Cozette ★(audio/international)
Tortured ★(audio/international)
The Pleasure Garden ★(audio/international)
Winter's Desire ★(audio/international)
Dark Pleasures ★(audio/international)

Made in the USA
Monee, IL
28 March 2021